THE BLIZZARD

To Jyl

I miss you so much.

"Our love forever."

Acknowledgements

My unending gratitude to my parents, Arthur and Ruth Blenski, for giving their six children a love for a reading, teaching us a solid work ethic, and for their sacrifices in sending us all to parochial school. How different might things have been without that discipline and educational foundation.

Profound and eternal thanks to my wife, Jyl, for her proofreading, sometimes brutally honest comments, and unfailing encouragement. She was always my cheerleader, number one fan, and best friend but, sadly, succumbed to cancer before this book was published.

Thank you also to my Mom, my brother Phil, my sister Betty, Jyl's daughter Danielle, teachers all, and my friend Chris Hoover, for their comments, suggestions, and proofreading.

For the patient and unflagging support of my good friend Peter Lampkins who was involved in so many phases of getting this book written and published, I will always be indebted.

Thank you, too, to Christopher Sennes and Ellen Mead for their involvement.

My good friend Dave Williams is always there for me and this project was no exception. Add it to that stack of IOUs!

The encouragement of my friend, former colleague, and published author Tom Basinski was always inspirational.

A very special thank you to my friend and former colleague Steve Casey, retired journalist, publicist, and law enforcement officer, for his "extremely valuable, insightful, incredibly brilliant comments" that kept me going in the early stages and laughing to the end.

Any hint of authenticity as it relates to the Marine Corps life of the protagonist's father, including uniforms, weapons, aircraft, bases and base life, is due to the input of Colonel Rodger

Harris, USMC (Ret.), Major Christopher Hage, USMC-R, former USMC Captain Peter Swicker, and Master Sergeant Timothy K. Whiteman, USMC (Ret.). I am proud to call each of them friend.

Lastly, but no less important, I am grateful for the outstanding work of my editors, Stephanie Seifert-Stringham and Erinn Martins.

FOREWORD

Adolescence is a time of conflict and confusion for most young people. Teen friendships and love relationships are transitory; there is pressure to achieve, to "fit in," be popular and attractive. Many adolescents do not hold themselves in high regard, and the absence of self-worth can be a serious handicap, which makes them more vulnerable to negative peer pressure, early sexual activity, drug and alcohol abuse, and violent and aggressive behavior. As parents and concerned citizens we are appalled and confused at the tragic violent outbursts in our schools around the country. We cannot ignore these cries for help. If we do, we are "selling out" our future.

The Blizzard by Marty Martins with its story of teenage peer pressure and young romance will intrigue and inspire young people everywhere. The hero, Chet, is a young man I think many girls would choose as a boyfriend. He is a role model for how young men should treat women in a romantic relationship. Chet honored and respected Melanie's decision to be abstinent until marriage. Melanie is a role model for many of our young girls today. Popular and pretty, she chose to go against the norm of her crowd and to maintain her dignity and self-respect. Anyone who ever went to high school has known a tough guy like Tommy. He thinks he has to prove his masculinity through sexual conquests. Of course he sets his sights on the good girl. When Tommy gets Melanie in a vulnerable situation and she rejects his advances, he reacts with fury. Girls today need to be aware of the danger signs of emotional bullying and possessiveness as possible (red flags for dating violence.

Of great concern to parents and educators is the increase in bullying and teen and college dating violence. Three recent and highly publicized stories regarding suicide of Phoebe Prince who faced unrelenting bullying from fellow pupils, the murder of Yeardley Love at the University of Virginia as a result of dating violence and the murder of nineteen-year-old Siohban Russell of Oakton, Virginia by her eighteen-year-old boyfriend demonstrate the need for more education for students, parents, and teachers to know how to recognize the signs of victimization and dating violence.

As reported by *Child Trends*, one out of every 10 high school students has been a victim of dating violence and nearly 10% of students nationwide had been hit, slapped, or physically hurt on purpose by their boyfriend or girlfriend. This research confirms the correlation between teen violence[1], sexual activity and substance abuse. Both girls and boys are significantly more likely to be victims of dating violence as they age.[2] Past estimates of physical and sexual dating violence among high school students typically range from 10% to 25% - even higher estimates are found when verbal threats and emotional abuse are considered. Adolescents who engage in drinking alcohol or using drugs are more likely to engage in or be victims of other destructive behaviors, such as teen sexual intimacy and violence.

According to a 2009 Justice Department survey of children 17 or under:

- 40% of teenage girls 14-17 know someone their age who has been hit or beaten by their partner.
- Nearly 80% of girls who have been physically abused in their intimate relationships continue to date their abuser.
- 38% of date rape victims are young women between 14 and 17 years of age.

---

1   http://www.safeyouth.org/scripts/faq/bullying.asp

2   www.childtrendsdatabank.org; Dating Violence

Marty Martins eloquently makes the case in his novel, *The Blizzard,* that adults must roll up their sleeves and get involved with their own adolescent children and other young people. Reasoning ability and emotional stability are often still immature among many adolescents. Despite protests they need an abundance of awareness and involvement of the adults in their lives. The code of silence among many teens has led to destructive and tragic consequences. Parents and youth programs must penetrate this code and work to eliminate the lack of awareness and inaction in regard to bullying and violence among young people. As a tribute to the lives of Phoebe, Yeardley and Siohban attention must be paid to this growing tragedy. If only they had a hero to protect them. Our girls must learn to be less vulnerable and our boys must learn to be more protective. If we take action as adults to encourage this learning our teens will lead happier and safer lives. *The Blizzard* is a means of starting an important and possibly life-saving dialogue with our young people – our leaders of tomorrow.

Elayne Bennett
Founder & President
Best Friends Foundation

MANŌ PA'ELE  **PUBLISHING**

San Diego, California

Cover photo by Peter Lampkins. *Cover design by Frank Fung.*

ISBN 978-0-9845680-6-2

Library of Congress Catalog Number 2010900013

Printed in the United States of America
10 9 8 7 6 5 4 3 2

Prologue

Lieutenant Colonel Peter F. Buçek swirled the black coffee in his mug as he waited for his wife to join him at the kitchen table. The kids were still in their rooms, so the old yet serviceable house was quiet. A tiny breeze moved through the screen door and kitchen window. Another humid North Carolina day was beginning.

Ellen Buçek returned the pot to the coffeemaker, opened the refrigerator long enough to pour a splash of milk in her cup, then sat down across from him and smiled.

"Thank you for last night."

"Thank *you*," he said with a smirk. They sat and grinned at each other, reliving the moment.

Bias aside, Ellen thought her husband a handsome man, but as she admired him sitting there in his Service C uniform - green trousers with khaki web belt, a short-sleeved khaki shirt with an open collar revealing a bit of the neckline of an immaculate white T-shirt, and mirror-polished black shoes - she wondered, *Is there any man who doesn't look good in a Marine Corps uniform?*

"Honey, are you sure you want to do this?"

"Yes, I've prayed about it and given it a lot of thought. Now is the time."

"I'd feel a lot better knowing you were here on base in military housing while I'm gone. It's secure, you've got the

Exchange nearby, the kids could stay in the same schools another year..."

"Peter, I've moved all over the world for you. The children and I have made sacrifices for your career - not that I'm complaining, I'd gladly do it over again - but you promised me when we got married you'd retire after twenty years. Now, with a little over a year to go, you're being sent to a combat zone for the first time. Okay, orders are orders, but while you're gone, I don't have to wait for you on a Marine base.

"I love that farm. My grandma knew I did. That's why she left it to *me* over all the rest of the family. When I was a kid, I spent every summer there. For years, all our Thanksgivings and Christmases were there, too.

"Well, *it* will be a great place to finish raising the kids and a nice home for our retirement," agreed Peter.

"The mortgage is paid off and there's not that much to do. Grandma leased most the acreage to the neighboring farmers years ago."

"I just never pictured us living out in the sticks."

"It's not even four miles to town! And you always said how you liked the small town atmosphere, the diagonal parking, even its tiny boulevard in the Village."

Peter watched his wife's brown eyes dance as she described the place, knowing further discussion was useless, but still enjoying listening to her talk about her dream coming true.

"Remember how you said everyone in town seemed so friendly even though you were a stranger? And Rockford is less than an hour away."

"Yes, I remember. Do you remember how cold the winters in northern Illinois can get?"

"Do you remember how hot it was in some of the places we went with you?"

Carnies beckoned from both sides of the midway, trying to lure anyone into a game. One even whistled at Alexis, who took one look at the man's wrist-to-shoulder tattoos and mumbled, "Gross!"

"Come on, Chet, let's go," she said.

"Just ignore them. I want to stop for a little while."

Chet pretended to watch some college-age guy trying to knock down three solid metal objects shaped like pint milk bottles. In reality, he looked to see what Melanie and her girlfriends were doing as he decided how to approach her.

He saw that Melanie and her friends were two booths down at the shooting gallery, talking to three big guys they seemed to know. It was obvious the one in the tank top spent a lot of time in the gym. The biggest one, the fellow with his cap on backwards, smiled or laughed at whatever Melanie said, then handed some money to the man running the booth. Chet watched the guy shoulder the .22 rifle and lean on the counter to steady his aim, then heard the muffled report of the weapon eight times. When the big guy finished, the operator handed the shooter a blue plastic lei, which he, in turn, proudly placed over Melanie's head.

"Come on," Chet told his sister and brother, who had started watching another sucker trying to knock over the metal bottles.

The small group was still chatting when the three Buçeks got to the shooting gallery.

"Hi, Melanie!" He could tell from her expression that she couldn't place him. "Chet Buçek from your math class." He pronounced the first syllable of his surname to rhyme with few.

"Oh, hi," she said, slightly taken aback at being greeted by a relative stranger, though one of her friends recognized him.

The other friend was checking out the new kid, his ruddy face topped with thick, sandy hair that curled over his ears.

"You go to our school?" asked the big guy with the backwards cap.

"I guess so, if you go there, too."

"I haven't seen you around before."

"We just started this week," Chet said, indicating his sister. "This is my sister, Alexis, she's a sophomore, and our brother, Brad."

"Guys, this is Chet...what did you say your last name was again?" Melanie asked, slightly embarrassed she had forgotten.

"Buçek," he replied without any tone of reproach.

"Chet, this is Tommy Schmidt, and Ted Allen, and Brian Hightower. They're all on our football team."

Chet shook hands with Ted and Brian, but Tommy just nodded without extending his hand.

Reading the body language, Chet guessed what was going on and ignored it.

"Can I win you a prize, too?" he asked Melanie.

She smiled and hesitated for a moment. "I suppose," she said, slightly uncomfortable after seeing Tommy's reaction. "If you want to try."

Chet turned to the carnie running the booth, a skinny twenty-something with bad skin and half of one front tooth broken off. An unlit cigarette was tucked behind his right ear.

Chet examined the prizes hanging from the sides and top of the booth. The largest were black-and-white giant panda bears with red bows around their necks.

"How many balloons do I have to break to win a bear?"

"Twenty five."

"How much does each turn cost?"

"Three bucks for eight shots."

"What will I do with the extra seven shots?" Chet asked.

Tommy and his friends started guffawing and mocking Chet for his bravado. "Yeah, like you're not going to miss at all?" one asked sarcastically.

Melanie's friends were giggling and teasing her for getting caught in the machismo being played out.

"Nah, I'll probably miss one," replied Chet confidently.

"You can do it, Chet," encouraged Alexis.

"Come on, Chet. Do it; win the bear," added Bradley.

Chet handed the man twelve dollars.

"I'll reload you after each turn."

"That's fine," said Chet, not wanting to change rifles once he started. He leaned over to his brother and quietly said, "Brad, watch where the first round hits. I'll try that yellow one in the middle first."

"Okay," Brad said, taking a position just behind and alongside his big brother.

Chet leaned down so both elbows were on the bench and lined up the center of the balloon in the sights. He had learned, the hard way, at a fair in North Carolina that the carnies often altered the sights just a bit so the barrel was off. It caused the shot to go wild, contrary to what the sights seemed to indicate.

He slowly exhaled the breath he was holding and squeezed the trigger. He heard the report and felt the tiny recoil on his cheek, but the balloon remained whole. He turned around and looked down at Bradley.

"Left."

Chet resumed his position on the bench, sighted the right edge of the same balloon, and fired.

POP!

Alexis, Brad, and some female voices all cheered. Chet couldn't tell if one of them was Melanie, but he hoped so.

He fired another round from the bench and broke another balloon. Confident he had the weapon sighted in, however wrong it was, Chet stood erect, right elbow up, left elbow down, and emptied the magazine to the demise of five more balloons. A crowd had started to gather, and with each successive hit, a cheer arose.

Chet turned around for a quick look at Melanie while the man reloaded the rifle but kept an eye on the carnie to make sure he didn't mess with the sights. On the contrary, Chet's success was pleasing the gallery operator as it drew in a new wave of potential customers who all thought they could do as well.

After Chet took out the next eight balloons in order, he turned around again. He got a little smile from Melanie that was hard to read. Even Tommy's friends seemed to be somewhat impressed; he heard one of them cheering for him. The scowl on Tommy's face told a different story.

The back board held thirty balloons, and only five were left when Chet finished. He accepted the compliments about his shooting from several fairgoers and handed the rifle to Brad, who was already onto the sight picture. The youngster drew big cheers from the now-large throng at the booth as he took the last five balloons without a miss.

The booth operator gave Brad a plastic lei, then began reaching for one of the bears with a long hook. Chet held up his hand to stop him.

The bears all looked alike to Chet, but he turned to Melanie and asked, "Which one do you want?"

Surprised that she was being given a choice, Melanie studied the array and pointed to one she liked. The man retrieved it and handed it to her. She thanked him and then turned to Chet, smiling, and thanked him, too. "You shoot well," she added.

Chet thanked her for the compliment. He wanted to capitalize on the moment and speak with her a little more, but just then, a tall, red-haired girl rushed up.

"Gigi, Melanie, Shannon," she said loudly, almost like she was taking roll call, "let's go! The concert's almost ready to start and I don't know how long that woman will save our seats!"

The four girls hurried off, and Chet watched Melanie leave, the bear over her shoulder and her ponytail swinging behind her.

"She's gone, Chet," said Alexis, bringing Chet out of his trance. "Do you have any money left for rides, or did you spend it all on that stupid bear?"

Chet just smiled, believing the bear, or at least winning it for Melanie, hadn't been stupid. "Nah, it was my own money I had saved up. Ready for the log ride, Brad?"

"Yeah, let's go. I'm hungry, too."

"Already?"

They had turned down the midway when a voice behind them, "Where you goin', show-off? I ain't finished talkin' to you yet."

Chet turned around and saw the big guy with the backwards cap, Tommy Schmidt, was addressing him.

"I didn't know you'd started."

The point was missed by Tommy.

"I didn't appreciate you buttin' in on my time with Melanie."

"I didn't know you had an appointment. It looked to me your time was over when all you won was that consolation prize."

Tommy's nostrils flared at the insult. Chet saw Tommy's two buddies had moved up closer behind him, all three having picked up on Chet's sarcasm. He had already sized up Tommy as about two inches taller and twenty to thirty pounds heavier than he, but Chet wasn't too concerned, especially if Tommy didn't know how to fight, but knew he hadn't a prayer against two, much less three, of them.

"Are you gettin' smart with me?"

"Come on, Chet, let's go," urged Alexis.

Chet ignored his sister and replied to Tommy, "It would be someplace to start."

Tommy moved closer and shoved a finger in Chet's chest. "Just stay away from her."

Chet felt his adrenaline rising, his heart getting jittery. He stepped back out of arm's reach, but his hands were already in fists in case this went too far. "If you stick your finger in my chest again, I'll break it."

Tommy stepped back and slid one leg back further so his body was bladed to Chet's, ready to repel a blow if it came.

The two boys stared at each other, each waiting for the other to make a first move.

"What's going on here?" demanded a deep, commanding voice.

They turned and saw two Winnebago County sheriff's deputies approaching. Chet opened his hands and tried to look relaxed.

"Nothin'," answered Tommy without taking his stare off Chet.

"That's right, officer, just a friendly discussion about the Bears and the Panthers," added Chet.

"It looked like more than that from what we saw. Break it up and go separate directions or go home, your choice."

"Yes sir," said Chet, nodding to Alexis and Brad to come along.

Before they turned away, Tommy gave him an ugly look that told him this wasn't over.

Chapter 2

Melanie got out of her sister's Honda Civic and opened the back door just as a gust of brisk October wind created a tiny tornado, swirling dust into her eyes, whipping her hair, and sending a spray of dried leaves into the backseat.

"Thanks, Mel. It might be old, but it's the only car I have," said Merrily as she reached into the backseat on the driver's side to retrieve half of the loaded Wal-Mart bags.

"Talk to Mother Nature. All I did was open the door," Melanie replied, lugging in the other half of the bags filled with rolls of black and orange crepe paper, cardboard witches, skeletons, and cats, and assorted other decorations, plus all kinds of party snacks.

"Where are you going to have the apple-bobbing contest?"

"The bathtub in the guest bedroom, so be sure to clean it tomorrow after you shower."

"Oh, thanks, a further price for accepting an invitation to your party."

Merrily laughed. "That's right. It's my seasonal twist on the old 'sing for your supper' rule." She looked over at her sister, younger by three years, whose nose and cheeks were red in the fall wind. "You look good in the Huskies hoodie."

"Yeah? Thanks, and thanks for getting it for me."

After two and half hours of work, the sisters stood back to admire the job they had done decorating for Merrily's Halloween party the next night.

"Pretty nice job, if I say so myself."

"Yeah, Merr, except that knocking down the real spider webs on your ceiling to put up fake ones seemed kind of a waste," teased Melanie.

"Real funny. Besides, there were only two. I don't have time to be checking for every little spider that decides to move in while I'm at school or work."

"Is it nice having your own apartment after living on campus?"

"Unbelievable. The freedom and the privacy are worth every penny. Sheesh, just to not have a roommate you don't always like is the best reason. I would have done it sooner, but you know Mom and Dad's deal."

"You mean the living in the dorms for the first two years?"

"Yep. You know you're going to have to do the same thing."

"Yeah, I know," Melanie admitted. "But I'm still glad you're close enough to come home on weekends sometimes," the unspoken part meaning she missed her sister.

"Thanks. Me, too."

"I can't wait to go away to college and get out of that one-horse town."

"I thought you liked horses?" Merrily asked, teasing.

"I do. I wish I'd never sold Quincy, but you know what I mean."

"Yes, there's a lot of world beyond the Village. Anyway, we'll work on all the food stuff tomorrow. Have a soda or something in the fridge. I want to show you my costume."

"Okay."

Melanie sat down with a strawberry-kiwi Snapple and began paging through a copy of *Cosmopolitan* magazine she found on the end table.

Before long, Merrily reappeared dressed as a belly dancer.

"Well, what do you think?" she asked as she held her arms out in a pose.

"I like it! You look great. Boy, you've really been working your abs! Yep, it will be a hit at your party, especially with the guys."

"I'm glad you agree. I thought so, too."

When Merrily came back out in her jeans and a Northern Illinois sweatshirt, Melanie held up the magazine. "Do you read this stuff?"

"Of course. There's lots of good articles in there. Fashion tips, make-up hints…"

"And the sex pointers?"

"Yeah, those, too. Plenty of good information a girl might never know or take years to find out. You ought to read them; you could learn something."

"I'm sure I'll have plenty of time to learn when the time comes."

"*Still* hanging on to your virginity?" her sister asked in a disparaging tone.

"Yes. Why wouldn't I?"

"You're probably the only senior in your school who's still a virgin, except some girls who'd like to get laid but can't find a guy to do the job."

"Merrily! That's not a very nice thing to say."

"Who are you saving that little flap of skin for, anyway?"

"My husband, who do you think? As if it's any of your business in the first place."

"Is having a bloody sheet on your wedding night that important to you?"

"Respecting myself and being with a guy who respects me is important to me. Not to mention..." Melanie stopped there.

"Not to mention what? Go ahead and say it; not to mention committing a mortal sin?" asked Merrily sarcastically.

"Yes, that too, of course."

"That's what confession is for," said Merrily, suddenly sounding defensive.

"Confession is for forgiveness as long as you *intend* to stop committing the same sin."

"Oh, God, Melanie, spare me your Sunday catechism bullshit!"

Melanie didn't respond.

Merrily saw the hurt look on her sister's face. After awhile, she said, "Besides, when I go to confession, I don't *want* to do it anymore. Things just get out of control sometimes, and it happens."

"And you think reading articles like 'Eighty-four Ways to Touch Him in *That* Place' doesn't plant certain thoughts in your head?"

"Well, if you're going to hook up, you want the guy to think you know something."

"And I'm sure the guy is equally well-read for the girl's benefit...not."

"They're probably reading *Cosmo* so they know what to expect," Merrily said, trying to make a joke.

When Melanie didn't laugh, Merrily went on. "In this day and age, guys expect it after you've been dating awhile. Besides, most the time it feels good."

"Oh yeah, those are good reasons. Right up there with STDs and getting pregnant before you're married."

"You can be as judgmental and as sarcastic as you like. What do you want? Am I supposed to sit home every weekend like you?"

"I don't sit home on weekends."

"Oh, that's right, you go out with your girlfriends because they don't have boyfriends either."

"They all have boyfriends or are dating different guys."

"Big wow. Who are you going out with?"

"Brady."

"Ah yes, the great Brady Walsh, your safe date since sixth grade. He's so infatuated with you, I'm surprised he didn't drive you here and offer to pick you up on Sunday."

"We always have fun together, and he never tries anything besides a good-night kiss."

"Are you sure he's not gay?"

"He's a varsity letterman! Backup quarterback on our football team and the starting pitcher on the baseball team."

"What? You think jocks can't be gay?"

Melanie didn't understand how the conversation had gotten turned around with her suddenly trying to defend her decision.

"It's not as easy as you think. Do you suppose high school guys are any different about expecting a girl to put out after a few dates? Like they spend a certain amount of money on you and you're supposed to go to bed with them? I'm not a prostitute!"

Now Merrily felt sorry for her sister, fully understanding the girl's dilemma.

"I'm not a prude, Merrily. I can get turned on reading a book or watching a movie just like anyone. Do you think I don't look at cute guys and wonder what it would be like to go all the way or to see buff guys with their shirts off, or the swim team in their borderline-obscene Speedos, and wonder what I'm missing and if I'm doing the right thing by waiting? But, in the end, I believe I am."

"Good for you, sis. I'm proud of you."

Melanie smiled back in appreciation.

"So that's it? There's no one else except Brady?"

"Gee, Merr, we live in Podunk, USA. I've known almost every guy since kindergarten. Gone out with most of them, at least the ones I liked and hadn't heard bad things about, *and who asked me out*, one time or another since ninth grade. Besides, once they find out I'm not going to go all the way, they quit calling."

"That's it?" Merrily asked, surprised that her pretty, genuinely nice, virginal sister didn't have some decent guy pursuing her.

"Well, there's this one guy, he just got here at the beginning of the year. Can you imagine having to transfer in your senior year? He's asked me out a couple of times, but there's just something about him that...I don't know, I can't explain it."

"Like what?"

"He's not like other guys. He's so self-assured and self-confident, it's almost like arrogance, but I don't think he means to be. And he acts older than everyone else; it makes me wonder if he got put back a couple of grades."

"He's not smart, then?"

"Oh no, I have him in three classes. He's very smart. But, see there, that's what I'm trying to explain. It's not like he's egotistical about it or anything. He's just like super confident he can understand or figure out whatever we're studying in class."

"And that's so bad?"

Melanie shook her head. "You'd have to be there. Here's an example. You know how the fair opens just before school starts? So my friends and I went. Tommy Schmidt, remember him?"

"Oh yeah, wasn't his dad the one who put his wife in the hospital and went to jail for domestic violence a couple of years ago? The gossip all over town was he'd been beating her for years."

"Right. Anyway, Tommy - one of those guys who *isn't* all that smart, but he's friendly enough - comes up and offers to try to win me something at the shooting gallery. You get eight shots per try, but he didn't hit all eight balloons and got this cheap plastic lei he gave to me."

"Well, it was a nice gesture..."

"Then this new guy comes up with his younger sister and brother and asks if he can win me a prize..."

"What's the matter with that?"

"Well, it felt a little uncomfortable, what with Tommy just giving me the silly lei and this guy I don't even know asking if he can win me something, too. I don't think he was trying to embarrass Tommy, but he did."

"I don't understand."

"He asks the man how many balloons would it take to win the grand prize, a huge stuffed bear. He misses the first shot, then proceeds to shoot twenty-five balloons in a row!"

"Wow, that's impressive!"

"Not to him, it wasn't. It was like he knew he could do it from the start. But there was another thing he did that wasn't like other guys."

"Oh yeah?" encouraged Merrily, wanting to hear more.

"The carnival guy went to get a bear from where they were all hanging above the shooting gallery. And Chet, that's his name, stopped him and asked me which one *I* wanted and let me pick it out."

"Is he cute?"

"So-so. Definitely not *bad* looking."

"But he asked you out twice and you shot him down both times. How'd you do it?"

"Just told him I had other plans."

"I guess he took your hint."

"Yeah, that, and then he saw me with Brady at Ficacci's after one of the games."

"Were you still in your cheerleading outfit?"

"Of course."

Merrily smiled, picturing the event. "Poor guy. So, who's dating him now?"

"No one that I've seen. He came to homecoming with a really cute girl, but she wasn't from our school. I never saw her before."

"Did he see you there?"

"Not that I ever noticed."

"Too bad. I'm sure you looked great."

Melanie smiled her thanks for the compliment and continued. "Oh, I nearly forgot. Let me tell you what did happen there."

Merrily was all ears. Whatever its drawbacks, small town America was not without its own drama.

"Everyone was out on the floor for a slow dance. The new guy, Chet, was dancing with his date and Tommy Schmidt was dancing with his date, Helen Krause. They were all real close to Brady and me."

"So, *you* were checking out the new guy while dancing with Brady?

"Was not. Just be quiet and listen."

"Tommy steered his partner right behind Chet then turned her real quick and he bumped into Chet. I'm telling you, Merrily, it looked like he did it on purpose. Chet and his date were really jolted. He turned around real fast to see who had bumped him.

"Tommy acted real angry like it was Chet's fault, even started taking off his jacket and asking Chet in a nasty tone if he wanted to step outside."

"What did Chet do?"

"He moved his date behind him and just stood there staring at Tommy. Keep in mind that Tommy is bigger and taller than him. Real slowly, he unbuttoned his jacket, but never took it off, and asked Tommy why he needed to go outside and challenged him to throw down right there.

"Can you believe that guy? Ready to fight at school, at homecoming no less, even if it meant automatic suspension and maybe expulsion!"

"Then what happened?"

"A crowd had started to gather, but even before chaperones got there, Tommy shook his head, then, real angry-like, said 'Watch your back, punk' and walked away."

"What did Chet do?"

"Finished the dance, then took his date over to the refreshment table. I didn't see him after that."

"Gee, nothing exciting like that happened when I went there."

Melanie laughed that her sister had enjoyed the story.

"Is this Chet out for sports or any other extra-curriculars?"

"Not that I know of, though I couldn't care less. I heard he played football at his last school but got here too late to go out for our team. Why?"

"Why? Because it might present an opportunity for you to let him know you're available, that Brady's just a friend."

"Did you hear anything I said? I'm not interested in going out with him."

"Okay, let me see if I get this straight: A smart, semi-cute guy who's not afraid to be seen at the fair with his kid sister and brother goes out of his way to impress you. He wins you a bear and even lets *you* pick it out. He's interested enough to ask you out twice, but you turn him down because he's self-assured and self-confident. In the meantime, you don't want to date any of the Neanderthals at your school but continue to go out with puppy-dog Brady, who, bless his heart, is someone you know you don't want to get serious with. Do I have that pretty much right?"

Melanie shook her head in resignation. "You don't understand. He's just not my type."

Chapter 3

"For homework, answer all the questions at the end of to-day's chapter. Be sure to show your work."

A communal complaint erupted from the class.

"Oh, I forgot, seniors want to be challenged," said Mr. Knopp in mock sarcasm. The teacher pushed up the rim-less glasses on his nose as he reached for the algebra book. "Let's see what else I can find..."

The class protested, louder than before. "Noooo!"

Eyes were already checking the clock above the whiteboard at the front of the room. Only two forty-seven. Maybe they'd get out early.

"No use wasting this valuable time. Let's have a quiz. Take out a pencil; all books on the floor."

Another group groan.

"Mr. Knopp."

"Yes, Miss Hondel?"

"I don't have a pencil," announced Melanie.

"Well, you can't take it in your usual purple ballpoint."

A number of students snickered, and several boys made smart remarks.

Melanie felt a tapping on her shoulder and turned, swish-ing her blonde hair across her back.

Her blue eyes met those of that strange new kid, Chet Buçek. Melanie returned his smile across the aisle and one seat back, accepted the pencil, and mumbled a thank-you. He's not that bad looking, if only he wasn't so weird, she thought.

Mr. Knopp slid one panel of the whiteboard sideways, revealing five questions. It was now obvious the quiz wasn't a last-minute time-filler by their math teacher.

"Be sure to show your work. Time ends when the bell rings. Begin."

Shannon, Melanie, Gigi, and Mary Frances met outside after school and headed down South Street, walking four abreast toward Center Road, their shadows long in front of them. Dry snow swirled across the sidewalk and danced around their feet. Each girl wore a bright pastel coat or jacket of a different color. The group looked like a live Crayola commercial. Gigi listened to her three friends complain about the no-warning algebra quiz, happy that she had been at band practice that period.

They turned north on Center Road and headed into the Village, as the town's small business district was known, pulling their knit caps or hoods tighter to keep their ears warm.

"Wanna go to Ficacci's or the café?" asked Shannon. The pizza parlor and McKaig's Restaurant were on the same block; the after-school crowd was pretty evenly divided between the two each afternoon.

"Oh, Melanie wants to go to the café," said Mary Frances. "Wrestlers don't eat pizza during training."

"What are you talking about?" asked Melanie, bewildered by the digression.

"Oh, don't tell me you don't want to bump into Chet and return his pencil," replied Mary Frances.

"And wrestlers have to maintain their weight during the season or they can't compete in their class, so Chet won't be at Ficacci's," said Shannon.

"Is he on the wrestling team?" asked Melanie.

"Oh, like you didn't know."

"I didn't."

"Probably because the cheerleaders don't support the wrestling team."

"Is it my fault they compete during basketball season, a sport people actually cheer at?"

"What's going on?" asked Gigi, feeling left out of what was likely a juicy story.

"Mr. Knopp announced a pop quiz and Melanie didn't have a pencil-" started Mary Frances.

Shannon interrupted. "Mr. Knopp, Mr. Knopp, I don't have a pencil," she teased in a mocking voice as she waved her hand in the air.

"Here, take *mine*," said Mary Frances in an adoring voice, extending her hand as she played the part of Chet.

"Shannon, your dad is waving at you."

"He probably thought I was waving at him. Hi, Dad," shouted Shannon, waving back across Center Road where her father was out on the lot of his Ford dealership. Not about to be interrupted, Shannon continued, "There's this guy in our class - you know, the one who won her the bear at the fair — he's been drooling over Melanie for months."

"He is not."

"Melanie, I sit behind you both. He can't take his eyes off of you. Don't tell me you never noticed."

"Why would I? The guy is weird. Wore those camouflage Army clothes all fall until it got cold."

"A Marine jacket from his father," corrected Mary Frances. "His dad's in the Marines."

"Whatever."

"I've only seen him with the jacket. Big deal, the rest of his clothes are normal," said Shannon. "It's not like he's a Goth or something."

"*And* the cap," said Melanie.

The others admitted she was right about the military cap.

"And what's with that tail he puts on the C in his last name, likes it's a Q or something?"

"Maybe it's like the C in façade?" asked Gigi, the perpetual peacemaker.

Melanie didn't bother correcting her.

"Ah, come on, Melanie," said Mary Frances, "You have to admit he acts a lot more mature than most of these small town guys."

"Yeah, I suppose."

"Probably 'cause he's lived all around the world on his dad's duty stations," suggested Shannon. "Okinawa, Japan; Rota, Spain; Diego Garcia; Naples, Italy..."

"My brother said he runs a trap line," said Mary Frances, not to be outdone as the source of hot intel.

"What's weird about that?" asked Gigi. "Other guys around here do that."

"Killing animals for fur is inhumane," said Shannon.

"Yeah," agreed Melanie without much conviction. "And what about last fall? I heard he trapped a hawk and trained it to hunt."

"Falconry is actually an ancient sport," said Mary Frances. "Does he still have it?"

"No, he let it go. He had to read his essay about it in English class. Said wild things should be allowed to stay wild."

"That's environmentally conscious," admitted Shannon.

"Most of those wrestlers are pretty buff," said Gigi, trying to maintain the positive tenor.

Again, there was consensus.

"Their uniforms are kind of sexy, too," said Shannon.

"Yeah," said Gigi, wiggling her eyebrows, "they don't leave much to the imagination."

Melanie rolled her eyes. "I wouldn't know, and I don't care, either."

Tired with that line of conversation, Shannon changed the subject. "You going to the sledding party this weekend?"

There was a chorus of "Oh, yeah!"

"Anyone going with anyone?"

"No."

"Nah."

"Me, neither."

"Then let's go together," suggested Shannon.

"Good idea," said Mary Frances. "Can you pick us up?"

"What, I'm driving now?"

The other three looked at her with expressions that ranged from "You had to ask?" to "What did you think?"

"Whatever," answered Shannon to her own question, rolling her eyes.

"What are you going to wear?" asked Gigi as the bell on the café door tinkled above their heads.

Tommy Schmidt sped, but not too fast, through the Village to the outskirts of town, which wasn't that far, toward the feed mill. He was going to be late for his part-time job. He spun the steering wheel of his pickup truck around corners while he held his milkshake in the other hand. Saturday might be the chance he'd been waiting for.

He had dashed into McKaig's after school to get a chocolate shake and had seen Melanie and her friends at the table near the jukebox. He had eased over to their table on his way out, trying to act like it was a casual encounter. As he'd approached, he had overheard them talking about sledding that weekend.

He had said hi to the girls, all fellow seniors. Of course, they were in college-prep courses, so he'd never had many classes with them. They had each greeted him in turn, even that uppity bitch, Mary Frances Flaherty. God, he hated her.

"You going to go to the sledding party at Kindler's Farm on Saturday, Tommy?" asked Melanie, the one who was always the nicest. Also, the prettiest. He knew she had a thing for him ever since she had started cheerleading in junior year.

"Hadn't thought about it. I usually have to work. You goin' to be there?"

They had all said they wouldn't miss it, although he didn't care. He had intended the question only for Melanie.

"I'll have to see if I can get off, but it sounds like fun."

"You were there last winter," said Shannon. "Remember how crazy it got? It'll be a blast!"

"Yeah, Tommy," said Melanie, "you should come."

Yep, that was it, thought Tommy as he skidded to a stop in the gravel at the mill, trying not to spill anything on his letterman's jacket. *Melanie gave me a personal invitation. She wants me to be there.*

"You're five minutes late!" said the mill owner in his usual gruff voice.

His father was at the controls of the mixing hopper, near enough to hear their employer's remark, and gave Tommy a dirty look. Tommy wasn't worried about getting thrashed by his old man, anymore. The beatings had stopped once he'd grown two inches taller and twenty pounds heavier than his father. But, he knew he'd either get chewed out once he got home or have to wait for a sarcastic remark in front of his mother at the dinner table.

"Sorry, Mr. Svensen. I got held up after school." *Better wait until later to tell him I need tomorrow afternoon off,* he told himself.

"Get those bags of barley loaded on Johansen's truck, but first carry these bags of Dog Chow out for Mrs. Miller."

As he walked toward the area where the small-animal food was stacked, Tommy's dad said, "Typical woman, she can put those two fat kids in their car seats and lift that German Shepherd in the back but can't load a bag of dog food."

Tommy hefted a twenty-five-pound bag under each arm and followed Mrs. Miller to her car, his mind somewhere else. *I wonder if Melanie likes Axe.*

Chapter 4

"Alexis, has your horse been fed?"

"Yes, Mother."

"Brad, did you feed the chickens?"

"Yes, Mommy. What's for supper?"

"Chet, you're not going to be late, are you? Your father is calling tonight."

"I know, Mom. I'll be here on time."

"Aren't you leaving later than usual?"

"Practice went long. Our last meet is tomorrow and we still have a chance for state. Don't worry, it's already staying light longer."

Chet finished tying his thick-soled rubber hiking boots, put on his parka and cap, pulled up the hood, and shouldered his Savage 22/20 combination rifle-shotgun.

"Come on, Belle."

The invitation wasn't necessary. The German Shorthair Pointer had been ready to go as soon as her master had put on his coat. His reaching for the rifle had just made her more excited; they weren't just going outside, they were going in the field.

Chet followed the fence line until he got to the back of their property, ducked through the sagging barbwire fence, and crossed pasture land on the Windsors' place before he got into the woods and made for the river. It was a small river, or maybe just a big stream, but it ran year round, meandering south and east before it met the larger Pecatonica. Chet headed upstream. The darkening sky was a dull gray. He knew more snow was imminent.

He had the location of all his traps memorized: a particular old tree, a rock unlikely to get buried in snow, a bent sapling near the shore. He didn't otherwise mark the sites. His dad had taught him that not all trappers are honest and would steal the catch out of another guy's trap and sometimes even take the trap.

At the first stop, Chet commanded Belle to stay, hung his rifle from the stump of a thick, broken tree branch, and walked to the bank. He brushed away some snow until he found the stake pounded into the ground. Taking the chain attached to the stake, he pulled the trap out of the water. Still set.

He checked to confirm there was still evidence of muskrat activity nearby, then carefully released the trip, removed the piece of carrot, and dropped it in the water. He pulled his right glove off with his teeth. From a plastic baggie in his coat pocket, he took a slice of apple, hooked it in the trap, and reset the device. After replacing his glove, he gently lowered the trap back in the river and brushed snow over the chain to hide it.

"No luck there, girl."

Chet again slung the rifle "African style" like his dad had taught him, stock up, barrel down, so snow and other debris couldn't fall into the barrel as he hiked.

It was almost three miles to the end of his line and he had harvested four 'rats by the time he reached that point. They were all good specimens with full winter coats and had been in the water less than twenty-four hours.

Some other time, he might have stopped at the old shack near the end of his line. Someone had built the little cabin years ago, maybe for a hunting camp. Now it was nestled, almost hidden, in a stand of aspen that had grown up around it. He liked going there to get out of the wind and maybe even start a fire in the old stove to warm up before starting back. But he couldn't do that tonight. As inviting as warming up sounded, he was getting hungry and didn't want to miss talking to his dad.

"Okay, Belle, we better double-time it back or Mom will have my hide."

The dog's ears went up as he talked, then she ran out ahead of him.

As soon as the dinner dishes were washed, dried, and put away, they gathered around the home's only computer to see the head of their family. They pulled chairs from the table tightly together so the little camera mounted on top of the monitor would catch them all in the same view. The children had noticed some time ago that their mother always brushed her hair and dabbed on her favorite perfume before these long-distance visits bounced off some satellite between Illinois and Afghanistan.

Brad had already logged on to the videoconferencing Web site maintained by the base MWR, or morale, welfare, recreation office in Kabul. A Marine who had been talking to his family someplace in Texas got up from the chair, and their dad was right there to sit down.

"Hi, Dad."

"Hi, honey."

"Hi, sweetheart. Hi, kids. How's everyone doing?"

"We're fine, Dad," said Brad. "We miss you."

"I miss you all, too. So, Alex, how does Buckwheat like the cold weather?"

"Buckshot, Daddy!" she said with a smile and a roll of her eyes at the familiar joke "Except that he looks more like a musk ox or something with his winter coat, he's fine."

"Dad, there's a beaver dam just beyond the end of my trap line!"

"That's great, son! Have you seen any?"

"Not yet. Plenty of sign and lots of trees down. The river is backed into a nice, small lake behind it."

"Should mean some good fishing this summer."

"Yep."

After listening to a report from each of his children, with comments or corrections from his wife, Lieutenant Colonel Buçek said, "I have some news, too."

"What is it, Dad?"

"Yes, honey, what is it?" asked Mrs. Buçek, both curious and concerned.

"I'm getting the Bronze Star with a V."

Ellen Buçek hadn't been a Marine wife for two decades without knowing something about military awards and decorations. She knew the "V device" was only added to that medal for combat heroism.

"The Bronze Star for Valor? What did you do, Peter?" she demanded more than asked. Her worst nightmare was of a Marine in dress blues on one knee handing her a tri-fold flag.

"Just one of those flare-ups you get caught in every now and then."

"What happened, Dad?"

"I went out with a unit to a forward operating base. Had to get an NCO to sign some papers for an uncontested divorce and child support, and check with the troops about some other legal issues.

"I was at a desk in the camp HQ, and all hell broke loose. The Afghan police station next door took some rocket-propelled grenade rounds, which was the start of a Taliban offensive. Their main target, though, seemed to be the school for girls on the other side.

"I put on my helmet...yes, honey, I was wearing my body armor...grabbed my rifle, and got out quick. I thought our building was next and jumped into the nearest bunker. The Muj - that's the shorthand they use over here for mujahadeen, the Taliban fighters, - were advancing from rock to rock in a wide semicircle on our front and flanks. Fortunately, the geography made it hard for them to get behind us.

"Our convoy was still parked outside. The kid on the .50 in our middle Humvee was as cool as a cucumber and just laying 'em down like hay in front of a mower. The Marine operating the Mk 19, that's the automatic grenade launcher, on the forward Humvee wasn't so lucky."

"What about *you*?" said Ellen Buçek, wanting to hear that her husband was not wounded.

"The fella next to me took some shrapnel in the face. He's going to be fine; didn't get his eyes, either."

"Peter!"

"I'm getting to it, Sweets. I picked up his SAM-R, that's an M16 with a heavy barrel and this great scope, and I just started pickin' 'em off. It was almost like I knew which one would pop up next. I was in the bunker, just plinking away, didn't even realize two guys next to me both went down with wounds. They're both going to make it. Finally, the Taliban took off. Probably picked up radio traffic that air support was coming."

Ellen Buçek breathed an audible sigh of relief and said a silent prayer of thanksgiving.

"How many did you get, Dad?" asked Chet.

"Not enough for the three Marines we lost. They said I may have gotten more, but they credited me with nineteen."

"Wow!" exclaimed Brad.

"Nice shooting, Dad," said Chet.

"Yeah, Daddy," agreed Alexis.

"But you're okay?" asked Ellen, wanting further confirmation.

"Yes, sweetheart, I'm fine. I can't say the same for the Taliban. Hopefully, they'll think twice before they return. Anyway, I saved the best 'til last."

"What is it, Daddy?" asked Brad, expecting more heroic action.

The Marine waited, wanting his wife to ask, too.

"What else did you do?" she inquired, her eyes narrowing to little slits. She saw him smile because he had gotten her to respond.

"Nothing else, love. Just that I get to come home for two weeks plus four travel days!"

There was a moment's delay while the announcement sank in, then pandemonium reigned for a good minute as everyone screamed, laughed, and cheered.

"When?"

"I should be on the next C-17 returning to Kuwait. Then I'll be on the next plane out, either hopscotching across Asia and Europe or Okinawa to Hawai'i."

"We can't wait to see you, honey. I miss you."

"Yeah, Dad. Maybe you'll be back in time to catch the state tournament if I qualify."

"You will, Chet, count on it. I can't wait, either."

"Okay, kids, you're all excused," said their father. It was his usual ending to their part of the visit. Now they had to clear out of the dining room so Mom and Dad could have some time alone. They left, pulling the old pocket doors closed behind them.

"Peter, I hope you're not volunteering to go out with those convoys or patrols or whatever it was, just so you can see some action."

"No, Honey, I'm not. I'm just doing my job, which sometimes means going out to the forward posts."

"I don't know why someone else can't just take the papers and get the signatures."

"So, it's okay if someone else is taking the risk to do my work, not to mention being unable to answer any legal questions that may come up?"

She heard the irritation in his voice and knew better than to question his ability to carry out his duties. "No, that's not what I meant."

"Thank God it's not like Iraq, where nearly every unit pretty much had a JAG officer in their pack to lecture them about the rules of engagement before every operation."

"Peter, I just don't want anything to happen to you. I don't want to think of my life without you in it."

"Sweetheart, I love you. I love the kids. I'm here to do a job, but I'll be glad as you when it's over."

"I miss you, Peter."

He heard her tone and understood the full meaning, a sentiment he shared. "I miss you, too, Angel. I've got to go, but just think, in a few days I'll be with you for two weeks! You'll probably get tired of me."

The lump in her throat was too big to say more than "bye" and blow him a kiss.

"Where are you going?" asked Ellen when she came back into the kitchen and saw Chet in the back hallway, putting on his boots and coat again.

He caught her still wiping away tears as she often did at the end of the satellite calls.

"I have to skin and stretch some 'rats I brought home tonight."

"Don't stay up late. You have a meet tomorrow."

"I know, Mom. I won't. Come on, Belle."

After making sure the house was locked up and her children were in bed, even if two of them still had their reading lights on, Ellen Buçek got herself ready for bed.

She hadn't gone into town or had company that day, so she didn't have any makeup to remove; she just washed her face and applied moisturizer, then changed into her nightgown.

It was late, so she decided to say her prayers in bed. After she had gotten under the sheets and pulled up the down comforter, the night's phone call intruded on her thoughts. The more she dwelled on it, the angrier she became.

It was so unfair. Yes, she admitted, she had known what she was getting into when she married a Marine. She had packed and unpacked their furnishings more times than she could remember. She had moved around the States and to four foreign countries to his different duty stations, making a home for them each time and sometimes working outside the home, besides.

She had borne three children for him along the way and, she knew, would have happily had more, but for the bout with cancer six years ago. Only once had she been close enough for her mother or sisters to come and help her when she had come home from the naval hospital with a new baby. Yes, the other

Marine wives always had been supportive, but that's the way it was. Who else did they have? Which was another thing: She never had a chance to develop any real girlfriends. The life was too transient for that.

Then there was the whole pecking-order nonsense the officers' wives had to mimic in their social lives, mirroring their husbands' positions in the chain of command. Did she ever complain about that or fail to help those below her or show deference to those above?

Yes, he is a Marine who can still run with the newest PFC fresh from boot camp and still shoot Expert at every qualification, but why now, God? He's a lawyer, for goodness sake. Why now, when he is so close to retirement, is he putting himself in danger, letting himself get in the middle of a firefight?

She pulled his pillow to her and hugged it. *How selfish can he be? Does he think it's easy taking care of the children and animals and maintaining the house and car by myself? I'm still young; what about my needs? Does he think I want to sleep by myself for the rest of my life?*

As soon as she thought that, a spirit of conviction overwhelmed her. *Who's the one being selfish? Didn't he dedicate his life to serving his country as well as being a husband and father? Didn't he share the responsibility for the Marines in his command while still worrying about his family while he was gone? After all these years, it was the first time he had to serve in a combat zone. Wasn't that a blessing, right there? Wasn't he also sleeping alone every night, in a faraway land, wondering if he'd wake up alive or be the victim of a nighttime attack? At least I have the comfort of our children and the safety of a warm home every night.*

She rolled out of bed and got on her knees. "Forgive me, Lord. Protect Peter. Get him back to us whole and safe. St. Michael the Archangel, defend him in battle."

Chapter 5

It had snowed all night and hadn't stopped. The Hondels' driveway, plowed that morning, was almost buried again in the middle of the afternoon. Shannon pulled up in front of the house and honked. As usual, she was driving a brand-new car with dealer plates.

"I'm talking to her on the phone, Shan!" said Mary Frances. "She knows we're here."

"Everyone will already be there," said Shannon.

"You're not going to be marked tardy, if we're the last ones," kidded Mary Frances.

Melanie came out the side door wearing a light-blue knit cap to match her pillowy down jacket.

"Where's she going now?" asked Shannon when Melanie turned toward her backyard.

"Here she comes," said Gigi.

"Oh, cool," said Mary Frances. "She got saucers!"

As she neared the car, Melanie yelled, "Pop the trunk." She tossed the large aluminum disks inside and slammed the lid.

"You're only wearing jeans?" asked Mary Frances after Melanie got in. "Won't you get cold?"

"Nah. I've got long johns on and sprayed my jeans real well with Scotchguard. Two pairs of socks and waterproof boots. I'll be fine."

"Look at Shannon's new ski clothes," directed Gigi.

Melanie could see Shannon's white woolen turtleneck and leaned over the seat to see her pink ski pants. Shannon pulled the matching jacket from the seat between her and Mary Frances and held it up. "What do you think?"

"You're stylin', girl," said Melanie.

"All this new snow is going to make the sledding at Kindler Hill great!" said Shannon as she hunched over the steering wheel, trying to keep them on the unplowed highway while silver dollar-sized snowflakes bombarded the windshield.

When they got to the Kindler place, more than a dozen vehicles were parked on both sides of the road. They saw recent arrivals heading in, pulling sleds and toboggans.

Leonard and Margaret Kindler had farmed here for more than fifty years. None of their children had wanted to go into farming, so when Leonard retired, they had sold off all the land except an acre and a half around the house and barn. Their backyard dropped off steeply toward the woods, and when it was covered with snow, the sledding was phenomenal. The Kindlers never minded the kids and families using their hill and even seemed to enjoy having the young people around as long as they didn't stay too late.

"Let's go!" urged Gigi.

"One of you want to carry the other saucer?" asked Melanie. "I don't care who uses them, just don't let me forget them."

Twenty or more young people stood at the top waiting to go while an equal number polka-dotted the hill in a splash of colors. The girls saw many of their classmates or other kids from their school, plus others they'd gone to grade school with who now attended Boylan.

The snow was coming down steadily, obliterating the sled tracks almost as fast as they were made. Melanie and her friends turned to find the source of a scream of laughter and saw eight kids zooming downhill on a toboggan. A spray of snow flew up before it as the curved front plowed through the powder. More shrieks came from the bottom when it seemed the toboggan would go straight into the woods but stopped just short of the trees.

"Here I go," yelled Melanie, jumping on the saucer and twirling downward.

"Me, too," shouted Gigi, close behind.

The merriment continued all afternoon. The sun, faint behind the snow clouds, was getting low in the southwest, and the snow continued to fall. It wasn't especially cold, thanks to the lack of wind, but everyone cheered when Kevin Jameson showed up with an Igloo beverage cooler filled with hot chocolate and a tube of Styrofoam cups.

Kevin also broke out a black plastic trash bag. "Cups in here, guys," he ordered. "We don't want the Kindlers mad at us."

The drink wasn't real hot chocolate made with milk, but the thin water-based kind. Still, it was hot, and everyone surrounded the Igloo until people were tipping it sideways to drain out the last drops.

"Hey, Melanie," shouted Mary Frances, "come on the toboggan with us."

"I'm warmed up now! Let's go!" Melanie shouted as she kicked her way through the snow.

It took the usual minute of coordination to get eight people onboard. Except for the person in front, everyone else had to sit down, scoot up, and wrap their legs around the person in front of them. Melanie was second last and big Tommy Schmidt, the high school fullback, got on behind her. She thought she'd get crushed when he wrapped his thick legs around her, then suddenly, they were zooming downhill.

Someone up front yelled, "Lean right!" Holding onto the ropes along the side, they all tilted to the right. "Lean left!" Then the other way. Back and forth they swayed, sending up clouds of white powder with each turn.

They tilted too far at the bottom. The whole toboggan tipped over, spilling out all its occupants. Melanie ended up on top of Tommy Schmidt. She looked down at his snow-covered face and saw him smiling back. "You can get up now," he laughed.

The octet trudged back up through the drifting snow, taking turns pulling the toboggan. They saw the crowd was starting to thin out as the sun set and the wind picked up.

"One more time," someone urged when they reached the top. Melanie saw Mary Frances talking to Shannon but was too far away to hear what was said. Mary Frances came over.

"Shannon is getting cold and wants to go."

"She's got the warmest clothes of anyone out here!"

"Who knows? I think we should get going."

"Melanie, you coming?" someone yelled.

Tommy Schmidt had overheard the conversation and stepped forward. "Come on, Melanie. You can ride home with me."

"Okay," she replied. She looked at Mary Frances, smiled, and shrugged her shoulders. "I'll call you tonight."

"Okay. Good."

Melanie was walking back to the toboggan when Mary Frances shouted back, "And don't worry, we've got your saucers."

Melanie caught the sarcasm. "Oh, yeah. Right. Thank you."

There were only six loading up this time, so it wasn't as crowded. A handful of kids were coming up, pulling sleds or toboggans, and it looked like Melanie and Tommy's group would be the last ones down.

They rocked the toboggan a few times to get it unstuck and away they went. No swaying from side-to-side this time, just straight downhill on one final banzai run. Maybe it was the fresh powder or the lighter load, but it seemed they were going faster this time. The trees were coming toward them lickety split. Could they stop in time? Roller coaster-like shouts of excitement turned to screams of fear from the girl in front. Melanie was looking over the shoulder of the guy in front of her and was getting scared, herself. It irritated her that Tommy was cheering wildly, seemingly enjoying this.

"Someone do something!" screamed the girl, thinking she was about to get crushed into an ancient elm.

Tommy grabbed the ropes, leaned slightly to the left, then threw all of his hundred and ninety pounds sideways the other direction, pulling up on the left rope as he did. The toboggan made a sharp turn to the right and tipped over again. There was total silence for a moment as everyone realized the possible injury they had just avoided. Then the nervous laughter and chatting started.

This time, Tommy ended up half on top of Melanie. He smiled down at her, then lowered his face and rubbed noses with her. She could smell mint on his breath.

She giggled. "Just like Eskimos," she said, trying to get up. He didn't move off of her. Instead, he leaned over and kissed her on the lips. It was a little surprising, but it was definitely a nice kiss she did not resist.

As soon as he stopped, she was embarrassed. She sat back up, fixed her cap, and stood up, brushing off the snow caked to her jeans, not looking at him.

Nothing more was said of the incident. They joined in the laughing and joking of the others as they fought their way up the deep snow on the now-deserted hill.

Fighting the stiffening wind, Tommy helped load the toboggan on the car roof of the kids who had brought it, then they trudged over to his pickup on the shoulder of the road.

"I hope it starts," said Melanie, "I'm getting cold."

When they were in the truck, she pulled back her hood and took off her knit cap. After shaking out her hair, she pulled the cap back down.

"No worries. The old Diehard cranks every time."

Sure enough, the engine turned over right away and they headed toward town, creeping along slowly on the unplowed road.

"If you're cold, slide over closer until the heat comes on."

Melanie felt funny about that. Unless there were three people in the front, only couples sat next to each other. Still, he was giving her a ride, so reluctantly, she slid over a little, but not right next to him.

"Want to try some of this to warm up?" Tommy offered a silver flask he'd removed from his pocket. "It's peppermint schnapps."

"No, thank you," she said, becoming slightly concerned.

"Are you sad basketball season is over?"

"No. Why?"

"You don't get to wear your cute cheerleader outfit anymore."

"Oh, well. Life goes on. I'll start college in the fall. My cheerleading days are over. What about you? What are your plans?" she asked, wanting to keep him talking.

"Well, I didn't get any scholarship offers, if that's what you mean."

Actually, it's not, she thought.

"Maybe I'll try out for one of the community college football teams."

"Okay, that's cool. And then what do you want to do?"

"I'll probably just end up working at the mill like my dad."

How sad, thought Melanie. *Even with an AA degree, he could do better than that.*

It was understandable he drove slowly, but she felt the truck slow down even more, then move over to a portion of the shoulder blown clear of snow.

"Is something the matter? Is your truck okay?"

"Kiss me again," he said, putting the truck in neutral and turning to face her as he unzipped his coat.

Instinctively, Melanie slid away from him until her back reached the passenger-side door.

"No!" she said firmly. "I'm sorry if I gave you the wrong idea back there."

"I know you like me."

"What? You're delusional."

"I saw how you watched me during the games."

"I don't think so!"

"And that time I made the winning touchdown against Stockton? You patted me on the ass."

"Tommy, half your teammates patted your butt, too. You think they have the hots for you?"

Melanie saw Tommy sliding across the seat toward her and became frightened.

"Don't be afraid, I won't hurt you. Take off your jacket."

Without even thinking about it, she felt her hand instinctively go to the top of her zipper and clutch it tightly.

He was closer, his right hand running through her hair.

"Tommy, don't do this. We're just friends from school."

He was almost in her lap. His left hand reached to pull her hand from the top of her jacket. His right hand had moved to her thigh. Tears of fright made everything blurry.

"Tommy, please."

As he tried to pull her hand from her jacket, Melanie jerked it away from him, and his left hand landed on her breast. It wasn't what he had intended, but he didn't remove his hand, either. Instead, he looked at her with a new lust in his eyes.

She slapped him. Hard. As hard as she could.

He pulled back, stunned.

"Bitch," he yelled as he struck her with a powerful back-hand across the face. Her head snapped back and struck the side window.

Melanie had never been hit before in her entire life and was amazed how much it hurt. She even saw stars, like in the cartoons.

Her dad had warned her about guys like this. She made her next move without even thinking.

She turned fast, grabbed the door handle with her left hand, and pulled it. The door opened and she fell out into the snow.

She felt more than heard Tommy getting out behind her. She ran for dear life, not looking back. She ran down the embankment along the road and out across a large open field. The wind had increased. The snow pelted her in the face. Her cheek throbbed, and her mouth was swollen where he had hit her. She could taste blood. It was getting dark and she only could see several yards in front of her.

In the distance she heard Tommy yelling. "I'm sorry, Melanie. Come back. I promise I won't do anything. Let me take you home."

The wind carried the sound of his words away, but she kept running, unable to stop, across the snow.

Chapter 6

Chet hadn't been out long before he wished he'd brought his snowshoes. The snow was falling hard, and the wind had come up, causing the dry powder to start drifting. He pushed on, though, anxious to check his traps before supper. He believed if a person was going to trap, he owed it to the animals to check the traps every day. That, and the fur went bad if you left them in the water too long.

The effort was already paying off. He had gotten muskrats out of the first two traps. There was none at the third, but the fourth set troubled him. This trap was anchored to the roots of a big tree that overhung the bank of the river. He knew the 'rats often came out of the water to eat on the shore and the drooping tree roots provided protection from any raptors ready to swoop down for a meal.

Trap four was set so it hung in the water on a likely exit from the river, but today it was on the bank. It held the partially-eaten remains of a muskrat. He crouched down, trying to decipher what had happened. He considered the two likely possibilities. Had the trap failed to make a good catch so the muskrat would die fast and the critter had climbed out onto the bank? Or had it already been dead when the other animal pulled it out for some easy pickings?

In either event, another animal had dined on his 'rat. There were enough tracks high on the bank under the tree roots to tell him it was some kind of weasel. Fishers were rare in these parts, so he guessed it was a marten. He reset the trap with fresh bait and lowered it into the water.

I wonder what marten pelts bring these days, he thought as he climbed up the bank. Once a marten moved in, it would start working the river from one trap to the next for free dinner. He threw the ruined muskrat carcass off into the woods for the crows and other animals to eat.

"No welfare kitchen for martens on this river," Chet told Belle. He opened the breach on his rifle-shotgun combo, made sure rounds were loaded, slung it barrel down on his shoulder, picked up the two dead 'rats, and hiked on.

The ankle deep snow with some drifts up to his knees was slowing him down. He knew he'd probably be late for supper, one of his mom's pet peeves. He could hear her now: "I don't go to all this trouble for you to eat cold leftovers." As much as he appreciated her good cooking, he always wanted to say, "But, Mom, that's what microwaves are for," but knew he didn't dare.

He could tell Belle was getting tired, too. Jumping out of the snow drifts every time she got stuck in one was wearing her out. He looked longingly at the line shack, barely visible through the white curtain of snow, when they went by. No time for a stop today.

When he finally got to trap ten, he pulled up another muskrat, quickly reset the trap with a slice of apple, and came back to his dog.

"Six for ten, girl! Not a bad afternoon."

Belle barked twice.

"I'm glad you agree. You ready for some chow? Let's go home."

He had wanted to go up to the beaver lodge today to check on any activity but knew he didn't have the time or energy, not with this storm.

Belle barked again and looked upstream, her ears raised.

Chet was instantly alert. He took the sling off his left shoulder, replaced it with the string of muskrats, and moved the rifle to the crook of his right elbow. Young though he was, he was woodsman enough to know to listen to animals when they talked to you. He knew how squirrels and birds announced his presence to one another when he entered the woods, but he understood his dog best of all. Someone may be coming, and in the woods, he couldn't be too careful.

"What is it, girl?" Was someone else out there, or was it something else? He pulled down the hood of his parka to hear better.

He thought he heard a voice carried on the wind. Belle barked again.

"Quiet!" he commanded, trying to listen. The dog obeyed, but he saw her ears go up at the same time he heard a voice...a woman's voice, barely audible, but crying for help.

Chet hung the string of 'rats in a tree and hurried in the direction of the sound, moving through the deep snow as best he could.

Then he didn't hear the voice anymore. Was the wind playing tricks on him? He stopped so he could listen in the snowy silence.

"Help me...please...someone...help."

It was more of a whimper than a cry for help, but definitely the desperate petition of someone in trouble.

Chet yelled back and kept yelling at intervals, not wanting the woman to give up, to know help was coming.

He homed in on the sound of the voice until it took him to the beaver lake. The buck-toothed mammals had built the dam where the river left open ground and narrowed on its way through the woods. The river had backed up behind the dam until it overflowed its bank and flooded several acres. Even through the blizzard, Chet could make out a person in a light-blue coat amidst the white, in the water twenty or thirty feet behind the dam.

"I'm here! Hold on. I'm coming to get you."

While he took a moment to consider how best to reach her, he propped his rifle on the top of a small pine tree nearly buried in a snow drift. It would take too long to traverse the top of the beavers' home. He knew the dam was a natural engineering marvel made of young trees, branches and grasses laced together and held in place with packed mud. It would easily support his weight but the jumble of snow-covered young trees and branches sticking out of the mound above the ice created an obstacle course. He was more concerned whether the ice behind the dam would hold him.

No time to think further. He started running across the lake, parallel to the dam. At least he'd be able to grab a hold of the dam if the ice gave way. The snow wasn't deep here, much of it probably blown away by the wind coming across the flat surface of the frozen lake. He got to the center pretty fast, but the woman, no, a girl - he could see now she was a girl - was still some distance away.

He pulled and tugged a poplar trunk out of the beaver lodge, got down on his belly, and started crawling toward her. "Hold on, I'm coming," he kept repeating.

She had stopped calling once she had seen him. Her powder-blue head was out of the water, two powder-blue arms spread on the surface of the ice, and the rest of her was immersed.

It seemed like forever, but he finally got to her. Chet extended the skinny tree trunk as far as he could while still maintaining a firm grip on it.

"Grab a hold of the pole."

She took it in both hands.

"Now just hold on."

He pulled with all his might, but she didn't budge.

"Can you pull at the same time I'm pulling?"

He could see her face straining along with the rest of her as she tried to pull, but it didn't help.

"I c-can't," she whimpered. "I'm too cold."

"Okay. Hold on. I'm coming to get you."

Chet slid slowly toward her, maintaining his hold on the trunk. "Grab it again and hold on."

He stood up and started hauling back on the pole.

He felt progress. She was coming out. Some of the ice in front of her cracked away, but he was pulling with all his might and before long had her whole upper torso out of the water and lying on the ice.

"Can you swing one leg up onto the ice?"

It looked like she was trying, but nothing happened.

"I can't feel my legs." Then she started to cry.

"Don't cry," he said. "The tears will freeze to your cheeks."

It took her a few seconds to catch the irony of his statement, and then she gave a little laugh.

As soon as he saw that smile, he recognized her.

"Melanie! It's me! Chet Buçek. You're nearly out. Keep holding the pole, don't let go."

He tugged even harder, feeling his arm and back muscles bulge inside his coat, feeling Melanie coming out of the lake. *Well, wrestling is good for something*, he thought.

If it had been summer, he would have guessed it was thunder. He heard a loud "crraaack," almost like a pistol shot, except longer, as he plunged into the icy water.

Chapter 7

"Alexis, where's Chet?"

"I don't know, Mom. He wasn't in the barn when I was there."

"Brad, have you seen your brother?"

"No, Mommy."

"Chickens fed?"

"Yes."

"Any eggs?"

"Six."

"Did you wash them?"

"Yes, ma'am."

"Well, wash your hands and start setting the table. Alexis, go outside and call for your brother."

Chet went completely underwater. When he touched bottom, he pushed himself back up, and luckily came up to the same hole he had fallen through and not somewhere still iced over. Once his arms were on the ice, he moved over next to Melanie. He didn't like what he saw. Her hair was frozen and matted to the sides of her head; her lips were blue. Worse, he saw the look in her eyes. They were dull and listless. She was giving up.

"Hondel!" he yelled where her ear would be under the knit cap.

She looked back at him, startled, but the spark was back.

"Where's that team spirit?" he asked, still shouting. "The team is down by two touchdowns, there are only four minutes left in the game! Give us a cheer!"

She attempted a smile, but it was a weak effort.

With one arm around her, he paddled to the point in the broken ice nearest the beaver dam. He reached down until he could grab the back of her pants under her jacket then pulled her up out of the water until she was lying on the ice.

"Melanie, you have to crawl toward the dam, toward those branches sticking out of the ice."

As soon as Melanie started moving, Chet paddled back to retrieve the poplar pole and returned. When she was far enough ahead of him, he held the pole on the surface of the ice out in front of him and swung one leg, then the other, up on top.

The pole helped distribute his weight on the ice until he had moved next to Melanie. He was afraid the ice wouldn't support both of them if he got her standing, so he rolled her over on her back.

"Cross your arms on your chest."

He grabbed the hood of Melanie's jacket and, on all-fours, crawled toward the shore, pulling her along.

Belle was waiting impatiently on shore where she'd been told to stay, although the tracks indicated she had been dancing around the whole time.

Chet slung the rifle diagonally across his back, got Melanie's right arm around his neck and his left arm around her waist, and started shuffling toward the line shack. It was their only chance. He could only imagine how cold she was, because he was shivering terribly. His hands, even in the wet gloves, were screaming in pain. Even with his knit cap pulled down and his hood up, he could hear the wind roaring.

The shack was less than a quarter mile away, but it took them at least fifteen minutes to get there. The last of Melanie's strength had given out soon after they had begun. Chet wrapped one arm around her back and the other under her legs and carried her, but he had to stop and rest often. Every step required pulling his leg out of deep powder and pushing it down on the next step.

It was also hard to see. The terrible wind howled as it blasted each tiny flake into a speeding dart, stinging the exposed portions of his face. He tried to keep his eyes open just enough to make out where he was going, but his eyelashes kept getting frozen together, forcing him to stop and use the back of his glove to rub them free.

The biting whirlwind cut right through his heavy winter clothes, now stiff with ice.

Several times he fell down, twisting sideways and cradling his precious load to his chest as he did, so he didn't dump her in the snow. He, too, was freezing, but he fought through the often waist-high drifts in the deepening nightfall, passing the muskrats in the tree, knowing it wasn't much further.

Snow had drifted up two or three feet in front of the small, one-room cabin. He had to set Melanie down so he could pull the rusty screwdriver out of the hasp holding the door closed. Belle raced inside. Chet picked up Melanie, carried her in, and used his back to shove the door partly closed behind them.

It took a moment for his eyes to adjust to the darkness inside. He was used to the stale, musty smell of the closed-up room, but it was heaven to be out of the wind and snow. Even with the gale blowing outside, it seemed as quiet as a mausoleum within the small structure.

Melanie was shivering violently. He got her sitting down on a chair, then went back to latch the door. He kicked some snow back outside but needed two hands to push the door shut. His clothes were crusted with ice that broke off as he moved around.

"Just let me get a fire going and I'll get those wet clothes off you."

No response.

"Melanie!" he shouted. "Did you hear what I said?"

"Uh huh," she mumbled.

He crumpled up some of the old newspapers stacked next to the firewood box and stuffed them into the pot-bellied stove in the center of the room. On top of that, he tossed handfuls of dry pine needles, then small twigs and branches as fast as he could break them up. Next, he put in two small pieces of firewood. He opened the old medicine cabinet someone had hauled here God knew when and took a farmer's match from the box. Striking it on the side of the stove, he held it to the paper in two places he could reach and made sure it caught.

Planning ahead, he pulled back the covers, a couple of moth-eaten blankets and a tattered but thick quilt atop old but clean sheets, on the bottom bunk - the only bed actually - of the sturdy, homemade bunk bed.

Kneeling before her, Chet untied Melanie's boots as fast as his trembling hands would let him, pulled them off, and then yanked off her socks. *Oh*, he noticed, *she's wearing two pairs*. He pulled those off, too.

He unzipped her jacket and tugged it off, first one arm, then the other, and tossed it aside.

The stove door was open, and in the yellow-orange light from the fire, he saw for the first time that her normally pretty face was red and swollen on one side, as was her lip. Dried blood was stuck to the outside of one nostril. He wondered if she had smacked her face on the ice when she had fallen through.

"Melanie, you still with me?" he asked, still talking louder than normal and giving her a shake.

"Uh huh."

Despite her response, he knew she was lethargic when he unzipped her pants. She didn't even react, not even a peep of protest. *Lucky you didn't*, he thought, *they're coming off anyway.*

He could hear the fire crackling behind him. He stopped to throw in some more kindling and another piece of firewood.

After he got Melanie on her feet, he had to pull the tight, wet jeans off over her round bottom before he got her back on the chair. Then he pulled off the jeans and her soggy long underwear and panties. *Hmmm, a real blonde*, he noticed, then felt guilty for even thinking like that.

He held her hair with one hand and pulled his other hand through it until he had removed all the ice and snow. Then he pulled the sweater off over her head, then a turtle neck, then an insulated long-sleeve undershirt. No bra, he saw. He felt guilty again for looking, for admiring her breasts. He hadn't seen many in real life, but these looked perfect.

"Okay, Mel, into bed with you," he said through his own chattering teeth.

He lifted her up and carried her shivering body to the bed, sorry he didn't have a towel or anything to dry her wet hair. He laid her down and pulled the worn covers over her.

He wanted to get out of his own clothes, but he had to make sure the fire was going well. He opened the door of the stove and saw that the wood was blazing nicely. He shoved in another, thicker piece of firewood. From the old, five-gallon paint can that served as a coal bucket, he scooped several pieces of coal with a bent garden trowel and dumped them in on top.

Before he got undressed, he turned the backs of both wooden chairs from the table, the only other furniture besides the bed, toward the stove. After wringing out Melanie's clothes as best he could, Chet draped her T-shirt, long johns, socks, and underwear on the chairs so they'd dry out. With shivering, aching hands, he got off his own wet clothes, surprised how rank everything smelled, and hung them wherever he could find a knob or hook, flipping some over the dusty rafters.

"Here, girl."

Belle came immediately. Chet picked her up and laid her at the foot of the bed. She started to sit up. "No! Lie down." She walked her forelegs out until she was lying down and watched him for approval. "Good dog. Stay."

His body shaking violently, Chet got under the covers and hugged Melanie next to him as tightly as he could. He could feel the body heat beneath her cold skin and briskly rubbed her back, arms, buttocks, and legs as far down as he could reach without letting her body separate from his.

"Ch-Chet."

"Yes, Melanie," he answered, overjoyed to know she was responding. And to hear her say his name, even with chattering teeth.

"My h-hands and feet feel like a million pins are sticking them."

"That's okay. It means they're coming to life. Just a little touch of frostbite. Put one foot between mine and the other one on top. Now stick one hand up here."

Melanie brought a hand up between their bodies, and Chet began rubbing it, hard at first, then slowly massaging each finger. "Put the other hand between your thighs for now."

When he finished with her other hand, he realized she had stopped shaking and sensed she had fallen asleep. He returned to hugging her body to his, relishing the warmth, and discovered that his own shivering was slowing down.

The Buçeks ate dinner without Chet. Alexis and Brad didn't say anything beyond small talk. They knew their mother was angry and frightened, a deadly combination for a sibling who got in the way.

Ellen Buçek moved the sliced potatoes around on her plate for the fifth time. "It's not like him to be this irresponsible. He's been late before but never missed dinner altogether."

"I'm sure he's fine, Mom," said her daughter.

"He could have had an accident with his rifle..."

"I don't think so, Mom. He helps teach the hunter-safety course for kids at the range."

"Accidents can happen to anyone," Ellen snapped. "Or he could have fallen in the river."

Neither child dared comment after that response.

"And look at that snow, it hasn't stopped since last night."

"I read a story about a guy that got lost in a blizzard in South Dakota just going from the house to the barn. They didn't find him until spring," said Brad.

Alexis shot eye-daggers at her brother.

"I'm sure it's nothing like that," said their mother, smiling faintly only because she realized the innocence of her young son's remark. But inside, another seed of fear had been planted. "Alexis, turn on the lights on the barn and the porch, then go turn on all the lights upstairs."

"Like a lighthouse, huh, Mommy?"

"Yes, Bradley, like a lighthouse."

Chapter 8

The outside temperature must have plummeted after sundown, Chet realized, because the stove was barely warming the place. He knew the little cabin was just plank walls with no insulation but had thought they'd start feeling the heat from the stove sooner than later. The wind was howling now, and he could hear thick tree branches banging into each other. The last thing they needed, though, was for that fire to go out.

He slid out from under the covers and discovered how cozy he'd become. The cold room shocked his skin as he danced across the frozen wood floor on tiptoes. *Thank you, Lord,* he prayed, when he saw coals and wood still glowing in the bottom of the stove. He gently put in two thick pieces of firewood and another trowel full of coal, then shut the door without clanging it.

He turned back toward the bed and stopped to look at Melanie. In the dark room, even the light escaping through the little isinglass window in the stove door provided enough illumination to see. Melanie had her hands under her head on the pillow, sleeping peacefully. The covers were pulled back just enough for him to see her long neck curving up to the start of her bare shoulder. Chet thought it was one of the most beautiful sights he had ever seen. He slipped back under the covers without disturbing her and fixed the blankets so she was completely covered.

"Where is that girl?" demanded Henry Hondel.

"Your guess is as good as mine," answered his wife.

"She's going to be grounded for a month! Where did she say she was going?"

"She went sledding out at the Kindler place with a bunch of the other kids."

"That would have ended long ago. Leonard and Margaret wouldn't want them there past sunset, anyway. Have you called her friends?"

"The Smiths' and the Thompsons' girls are home and say they haven't heard from Melanie. The Flahertys don't answer."

"Did she go to pick up Nancy? Maybe Nancy wanted to come home."

"No, Nancy's spending the night at her friend Heather's house, and both cars are still in the garage."

"Have you called Merrily?"

Ellen knew Hank was thinking of the time two years ago when Melanie had run away to her sister's place. "Yes, hours ago."

"What about Jack?"

"No, she didn't go to his place, either."

"Well, it's not like her to just stay out and not tell us where she went."

"No, Hank, she's *never* done that."

"You should have called her on her phone as soon as the sun went down."

"Henry Hondel, don't you dare start on me. I'm as worried as you are. You could have called just as easily as me if you were so darned concerned. And since when did we stop trusting her and start checking up on her every five minutes?"

"You're right, honey. We'll wait until the Flahertys get home."

Every direction Melanie looked, she saw snow. She was lost in the middle of a wintry nowhere. Pirouetting in a circle, she saw nothing but white, not a single thing to mark the landscape of the frozen wilderness except the blanket of snow.

Suddenly she saw a cloud of breath go past her, not her own. She looked over her shoulder, not even afraid, wondering who could be there. She shrieked. It was a huge polar bear. Where had it come from? How had it snuck up on her? It was pure white except for beady black eyes and a black nose, until it opened its gigantic mouth, revealing white, razor-sharp teeth in a blood-red mouth.

The bear expelled another cloud of steamy breath and slashed across the chest of her white jacket with long black claws that resembled five scythes. White feathers poured out and were blown instantly away. She began to run but couldn't outrun the bear. The white monster chased after her, reaching up with one paw and then the other, clawing at her and shredding her clothes. She felt her skin getting cold. The bear wasn't going to claw her to death; it wanted her to die of exposure. She fell down and waited for the bruin to pounce, to finish her off, but nothing happened.

She opened her eyes and saw a pair of rubber boots in front of her face. Her eyes moved up and saw it was a boy in a letterman's jacket from her school. He smiled down at her and held out his hand to help her up. She took the hand and was raised gently to her feet, still afraid to turn around. The boy unsnapped the front of his jacket, but after he took it off, he was entirely naked. He was pleasant to look at and she didn't feel ashamed looking at him. The boy didn't seem to be embarrassed about not wearing any clothes. He stepped past her and she heard terrible noises and a wild animal howl, followed by a bloody, gurgling sound. Still she didn't look, afraid of what might be there. The boy stepped back in front of her and took his jacket. She hadn't realized she was holding it for him. When he put it on, all his clothes returned, too.

"It's okay, you can look now."

Slowly, she turned around. There was nothing there but a large circle of red seeping into the snow.

The boy took her hand, smiling at her. He had a nice smile. "Let *me* take you home," he said.

Melanie felt cold and pulled the blanket up tight to her neck. Now that the aching chills had left her bones, the full realization that she wasn't wearing a stitch of clothes hit her. A sense of fear and immodesty raced through her mind and dissipated just as quickly. What could she put on, anyway? It was dark and she was under the covers. And Chet had been nothing but nice to her, not trying anything.

She sensed him getting back into bed and opened her eyes to check. She saw him smiling at her and smiled back.

"Mmmmm," she murmured, snuggling closer to the warmth of his body, feeling his arms around her. She finally didn't feel cold anywhere.

Ellen Buçek jumped when the phone rang. She grabbed it on the second ring, hoping it hadn't woken Alexis and Bradley.

"Hello."

"Ellen, it's me."

Even through the static of the satellite phone, she recognized her husband's voice.

"How did you know?"

"What?" he asked, bewildered.

Ellen quickly realized that he couldn't have known and was calling for some other reason. "Chet's not home..."

"Is he out on a date?"

"No, he went out on his trap line late in the afternoon and never came home. There's a terrible blizzard outside. We haven't seen him since before supper."

"You're sure the car is there?"

"Yes. I'm afraid he may have fallen in the river or had an accident with his rifle."

There was a pause as Peter considered her remark. "No, I'm sure he's all right."

"That's easy to say from half a world away. Why do you feel that way?"

"I just have a sense of peace about it. I've been hunting and fishing with that boy since he was a tyke. He's a careful hunter and a real woodsman. He may've gotten caught by the storm and holed up in a cave or a deadfall somewhere."

"There's an old cabin out there someplace. He's told me about going there to warm up sometimes. Took some old sheets out there I had in the boxes for St. Vincent de Paul."

"There, you see? That must be where he's at. He knew it was too dangerous to try to get home in a blizzard and spent the night there. Belle's with him?"

"Of course."

The Marine laughed. "Well, at least he'll have his dog to keep him company. Watch, he'll be home tomorrow morning some time. If he's not home by tomorrow noon, even if the storm doesn't stop, I want you to try calling me on my cell, okay?"

Somewhat relieved, Ellen said, "Okay, I will."

"Anyway, sorry for the late hour, but I called to tell you I should be getting out this afternoon. If there aren't any

SNAFUs, I'll make it in twenty hours. So I'll be home maybe late Monday, but more likely Tuesday."

"That's wonderful, Peter. I can't wait to see you."

"Gotta go, sweetie. I love you. Tell the kids Dad sends his love."

"I love you, too. I will."

She heard the phone disconnect somewhere in Afghanistan.

"Catherine? It's Sue Hondel. Melanie hasn't come home tonight, and we wondered if she was with Mary Frances."

"Golly, Sue. No, she's not here. We all went out to eat and to a movie after Mary Frances got home from sledding. She's in the shower right now. Can I have her call you in a few minutes?"

"Sure, Catherine. That'd be great."

Mrs. Flaherty could hear the shower running. She knocked and tried the door, but it was locked. "Mary Frances," she called loudly.

The water stopped and her daughter answered, bothered, "Yes, Mom."

"Melanie Hondel isn't home yet, and her folks are worried sick. I'm leaving the portable phone here by the door. Call her mother as soon as you get out."

"Yes, Mom."

After she dried off and applied skin lotion, Mary Frances, her red hair in a terry cloth turban and wearing her robe, came out and retrieved the phone. She was so used to speed-dialing Melanie on her cell phone, she had to stop a second to remember her home number.

The phone was answered in the middle of the first ring.

"Hello."

"Hello, Mrs. Hondel? It's Mary Frances. Is everything okay? My mom said to call."

"Thank you for calling, Mary Frances. Do you have any idea where Melanie is? It's going on eleven and she's not home yet. We're frantic."

"We went sledding at Kindler Hill-"

"Yes, I know."

"I came home with Shannon and Gigi, but Melanie stayed to go down again on the toboggan..."

"Yes?" Mrs. Hondel urged, wanting the girl to get to the point.

"So she decided to catch a ride with Tommy Schmidt, a guy on our football team. She said she'd call me tonight but never did."

"Do you have his phone number?"

"No, ma'am."

"Do you know where he lives?"

"Out in the country someplace. On a farm, I think."

"All right, Mary Frances. Thank you again for calling back. Good night."

"Good night."

Sue Hondel hung up the phone and looked at her husband, who had been pacing the entire time.

"She got a ride back from Kindlers with some boy from their school named Tommy Schmidt."

"Did she know his...?"

"No, you heard me ask."

"Where's the phone book?"

"Bottom left drawer of your desk."

Mr. Hondel stomped into his home office, jerked open the drawer, grabbed the fifty-page book, and slammed the drawer shut.

"A town of eleven hundred people, and a hundred are named Schmidt."

Sue Hondel knew he was exaggerating.

"How in the holy hell am I supposed to narrow that down?"

"Hank, watch your tongue. Let me see the book."

Sue ran her finger down the dozen or more Schmidt listings, at least half of which had Rural Route addresses, but none triggered her memory.

"Mary Frances did say the boy was on the football team."

The light went on!

"There's only one Schmidt on the varsity team, Tommy 'the Hun' Schmidt, the fullback. His dad works at the feed mill."

Hank sat down behind his desk and started flipping through his Rolodex, a duplicate of the one at his real office on Center Road. The mill owner, Gustav Svenson, was one of his clients.

He punched numbers into the phone. It rang on the other end for some time before anyone answered. Gustav was a cantankerous old Swede, and Hank knew he would not be happy.

"What could anyone want at this hour?" was the greeting. Gus spoke with a heavy Swedish accent and all his W's were pronounced as V's.

"Gus, it's Hank Hondel..." No response. "Your State Farm agent."

"Damn it, Hank. I know who my insurance agent is. It's almost midnight. What you want?"

"Gus, I'm really sorry to wake you like this, but I'm going crazy-"

"Yah. Only a crazy man calls people at midnight."

Hank ignored the interruption and the exaggeration. "Gus, my daughter didn't come home tonight. One of her friends said she was last seen with Tommy Schmidt, the son of one of your mill hands. What's that fella's first name?"

"Chip. Chip Schmidt."

Hank scanned the phone book. No Chip.

"Would you have his phone number at home?"

"No. Work records I leave at work." The word came through as "verk." "Did you look in the phone book?"

Hank was losing his patience. "Yes, Gus, I did. There's no Chip."

"It's not Chip in the phone book; it's his Christian name."

"Which is what?"

"Henry, Hank. Just likes yours." The old man laughed at the coincidence. "His real name is Henry."

"Thanks, Gus. 'Night."

Hank told his wife the discovery, found the number in the book and dialed. It was another long time before anyone answered, a woman it seemed.

"Ummm hmmm?"

"Mrs. Schmidt? This is Henry Hondel. My daughter goes to school with your son, Tommy. My daughter isn't home yet and someone told us she was last seen with Tommy."

The woman was wide awake now. "Are you saying our boy took your daughter?"

"No, ma'am, that's not what I'm-"

"Who is this?" demanded a man's voice.

"Mr. Schmidt? Mr. Chip Schmidt?"

"Yeah, who wants to know?"

"Mr. Schmidt, this is Hank Hondel, the State Farm agent from town. My daughter isn't home yet and a friend said Tommy may know where she went."

"Why would my boy know anything about it?" The tone was surly.

"I don't know if he knows anything. That's why I want to ask. He goes to school with my daughter and a friend said

Tommy gave her a ride. He might know where she went, or where she got dropped off."

"Why don't you just call him? Why am I paying for his damn cell phone if people are going to bother me, anyhow?"

"I'd be happy to call him if I could trouble you for the number," Hank said, trying to sound concerned and needy, when he really wanted to reach through the line and strangle the guy.

Mr. Schmidt rattled off the number so fast no one could have written it down, but one of Hank's powers after years as a salesman was the ability to hear and capture phone numbers instantly.

"Thank you, Mr. Schmidt. I apologize for waking you at such a late hour."

"Yeah, okay. I hope ya find your kid."

The line went dead.

Hank briefed his wife as he dialed, even though she had overheard half of the conversation.

The boy answered fairly fast.

"Hello?"

"Tommy? Tommy Schmidt?"

"Yeah?"

"This is Henry Hondel, Melanie Hondel's father." Hank thought there might be some response to that. There wasn't. "I'm hoping you can help her mother and me. We're really worried. Melanie isn't home yet, and her friend, Mary Frances Flaherty, said you gave her a ride from sledding at the Kindler place."

"Yeah, well sorta."

"What does that mean, Tommy, 'sort of'?"

"Well, she kinda got out before we got back to town."

Sue Hondel saw her husband's face getting redder by the second and could only imagine what the kid was saying.

Hank's knuckles were white as he squeezed the phone receiver. "Don't play games with me, Tommy. I'm a dad, my girl is missing, and I don't have time for games. What do you mean, she got out?" Where? Where did she get out?"

"I'm not sure. Somewhere out in the country on the way back from Kindler Hill."

"You let her get out on the open road in the middle of a blizzard?"

"Well, I didn't want her to. We kinda had an argument and she jumped out. I told her to get back in, but she just ran off 'til I couldn't see her anymore."

Hank couldn't take any more; he was having trouble breathing. If anything happened to Melanie, he was afraid he'd spend the rest of his life in prison for killing someone. He slammed the phone down and turned to his wife. "I'm calling the sheriff."

Chapter 9

It must have been the early hours of the morning. The bottom of the potbellied stove, glowing cherry red from heat, provided some light in the windowless cabin. Chet could tell the wind had died down, but the room was still frigid. He couldn't let that fire die. He tried not to wake Melanie. Sliding his bottom arm out from under her was the hardest.

Belle felt him moving and raised her head. "Stay," he whispered, reinforcing it with a hand command.

He hurried on tiptoes again to the circle of heat around the stove before he stood flat-footed. There wasn't much wood left, and even less coal. He quietly opened the door, used the trowel to put three or four more pieces of coal into the stove, and slid two smaller logs on top. He noticed one had a big knot in it. *That'll burn hot,* he thought. He felt the clothes on the chairs and saw they were drying well, so he shook them out and turned them all over so the damp side was up.

Melanie sensed Chet get out of bed and felt the dog move, too. She looked at him, at his bare backside, in the red glow of the stove. Other than accidently walking in on her brother one time, which she'd forced from her memory, she had always wondered what it would be like to actually look at a naked man. *Nice butt*, she told herself. As soon as he shut the stove door and started to turn, she closed her eyes.

As he got back into bed, she pretended to wake up as they wrapped their arms around each other.

"Are you warm enough?" Chet asked.

"Uh huh. I think I'm finally defrosted."

He smiled back, happy to hear her joking.

"Chet?"

"Yes."

"You saved my life."

He grinned, slightly embarrassed. For some reason, he felt it an overstatement. "Too bad I'm not in Scouts anymore. I would've received a medal."

"Don't act silly," she said, kind, not like a reprimand. "I would have died out there if you hadn't come by." She held his face in her hands and kissed him on the lips. Not a sexy, passionate, Saturday-night-make-out-session kind of kiss. Not a meaningless peck, either. She pressed her lips to his, softly, gently, and held them there. As she did, he felt her pulling her body closer to his. He realized he was kissing her back. Then, just as gently, she stopped. "Thank you." He felt her body relax and knew she was going back to sleep.

"Yes, Mr. Hondel, I hear what you're saying. Did you hear what I said? Have you looked out the window or listened to a weather report?"

When the panicky father didn't respond, the deputy sheriff went on. "We've got all the information. White female juvenile, seventeen years old, blonde and blue, five-foot-seven, one-twenty, last seen wearing blue jeans, a top of unknown color, a blue, down jacket with hood, and a blue knit cap."

"Light blue!" Hank Hondel corrected. "Light-blue jacket and cap."

"Oh yeah, my mistake. I had that down right here. Now, where was I? Oh yeah. Last seen in the company of Tommy Schmidt, a high school senior classmate. Reportedly got out of the Schmidt vehicle on a country road somewhere in the vicinity of the old Kindler farm around five p.m. Saturday. Do I have it all?"

"Yes," Hank said in resignation.

"Like I told you, she probably walked to a farm house and is staying the night with some family. Your daughter isn't the only person who got stranded last night. Contrary to common opinion..."

Hank Hondel could hear the sarcasm in the deputy's voice as he threw in the dig.

"Not everyone has a cell phone. The storm has knocked down a lot of electric and phone lines. There's nothing we can do tonight or until the storm stops. The snow plows will start working that area at sunup. We'll give her description to all of them. I just pressed the button that transmitted her description to all the sheriff's cars in the entire county."

"Thank you." Hank smiled to his wife, who was listening on the extension, nodding her head positively.

"Tomorrow we'll send a deputy out to the Schmidt place and have him talk to Tommy, see if he can narrow down the area where she got out."

"That would be excellent, Deputy."

"One other thing, Mr. Hondel. If it's anything like the last blizzard we had like this a few years ago when people didn't get home, any private pilots who go flying after the runways are cleared usually assist by keeping an eye out for marooned cars,

cars off the road, and the like. People are harder to see, but they report 'em if they spot 'em.

"That would be great."

"Go to bed, Mr. Hondel. There's nothing more you can do tonight. If anything comes up, we'll call you."

"Okay, I'll try. Thank you."

Melanie's parents both hung up, met each other halfway, and hugged. They were still worried sick.

Melanie stirred in her sleep. She felt something different in bed. When she was awake enough to realize what it was, she put her hands on Chet's chest and pushed herself away.

The pressure startled Chet awake, making him think something had happened. "What's the matter?" he asked. He opened his eyes and saw Melanie looking down under the covers, which she had quickly dropped when she saw him waking up.

Through the grogginess of sleep, Chet realized he had an erection and computed the chain of events.

"Oh Melanie, I'm sorry. I didn't know, I wasn't trying anything."

She smiled. He was cute in his embarrassment. "I know you weren't, Chet. It's okay. It just took me by surprise. Don't worry about it."

Chet felt his cheeks and ears get hot and knew his face was red. He wanted so much for her to think well of him and not that he'd try to take advantage of her in her sleep.

"I'm sorry," he repeated.

She touched his cheek, and he knew she could feel the heat. "Chet, I know how things work. Plus, I have an older brother and older sister."

He considered that for a moment and thought it was a little curious. "How does your sister figure into it?"

She laughed. "My sister's in college. She's told me more on purpose than my brother's ever shown me by accident."

Her hand was still on his face, and she felt him smile. She was glad he was no longer ill at ease. For some reason, the last thing she wanted was to hurt him.

"Besides that," she said in a conspiratorial whisper, "I read Victorian novels."

He'd heard about those and snorted a little laugh. He also realized she was staying on the other side of the narrow bed now. He missed holding her, feeling her breath on his face, and the smell of her skin.

She wanted to change the subject.

"My feet are thawed out. I have them under your dog."

"Good."

"What were you doing out here today? Or yesterday? I mean, lucky for me you were, but what were you doing? I didn't see you at the sledding party."

"I had a wrestling meet in the morning, went out for pizza with the guys, came home and changed clothes, and went out on my trap line."

Ha! He went for pizza with the team! Wait until I see that Mary Frances.

"So you really do trap animals, like I heard?"

"Yep," he said, proud to admit he did something most guys his age didn't.

"Why?"

"I sell the pelts to make money."

"How much?"

"That's kind of nosy," he said, teasing. Before she could respond, he added, "Ten dollars each, about three hundred dollars in a good winter."

"When do you do it?"

"You mean each day or the season?"

"Season."

"Coincidentally," he laughed a little, "it's right during wrestling season. Late October to the end of February."

"Doesn't it bother you, killing harmless creatures?"

"No." He paused, waiting to see if she would respond negatively. "I've seen you eating hamburgers. Isn't a cow or steer a harmless creature? You let someone else kill the cattle so you can eat meat; I kill animals for the fur. Is your animal product better because you let someone else do the killing part?"

She knew he was smart in school but was impressed the way he could explain his position even if she didn't agree.

"But killing for fur?"

"Is it different than your leather belt or leather purse?"

She laughed. "Did you rehearse this?"

"No, but it's something I think about. I don't kill animals just to kill, and I don't kill for fun. I kill to harvest a product just like the farmer or rancher. Wanna know something else? You'll probably laugh at me."

"What?"

"I thank the animal for letting me have its pelt."

She didn't laugh. It was kind of weird, but she thought it was touching.

When she didn't respond, he went on. "I read in a book that's what the Indians did when they killed animals, and I thought it was a righteous thing to do."

"My friends and I were talking about you the other day."

"Oh, yeah? And what did *you* say?"

"I said I hardly even knew you, and here I am naked as a jaybird in bed with you."

He snickered at the abrupt turn of events.

"I should try calling my folks. My phone is in my jacket."

"I know. It fell out when I was taking your coat off. I tried it. It's toast, probably from the water."

"Oh, well," she said, not too concerned. Then, after a pause, "I'm getting cold again."

She was already scooting toward him when he told her to come closer.

"I'll roll over so we don't have any more accidents like before."

"I told you, it was no big deal."

"Oh, now you're going to make fun of me."

She laughed at the unintended innuendo. "Stop," she teased, "That's not what I meant at all."

She snuggled up against his back, wrapping her arms around him so he was able to hug them to his chest. She was shivering again.

"Do you date much?" she asked.

"Not as much as I'd like. The girl I want to go out with keeps shooting me down."

Melanie smiled, knowing exactly what he meant. "Well, you shouldn't have given up so quickly." She paused for a moment, thinking. "Actually, now I wish I had gone out with you."

"But to answer your question, I date some. I just transferred here in the fall, so I don't know everyone yet."

"How come you never asked me out again?"

"I wanted to. Just about the time I got up my nerve to try again, you started dating that football player through most of the fall."

"It wasn't really dating. We're just friends, have been since grade school. We went together for a couple of months..." She stopped and chuckled at the obvious contradiction. "Back in seventh grade, but realized it was more pressure than just being friends.

"No, once high school guys find out I don't do it - and I always tell them on the first date - they don't hang around for too long."

She paused, anticipating a reaction. Chet rolled halfway back over, so he could see her, she guessed. She saw him looking at her, considering what she had just said, but when he didn't say anything, she went on. "I don't think I know anyone you've gone out with."

"Why would you? Direct line to Gossip Central?"

She laughed. "You're not like most boys, are you? Especially other jocks? They always brag about their conquests."

"Never had one," he admitted unashamedly.

"Never? Really?"

"Really. Besides, I don't kiss and tell."

He waited for her to laugh or respond, but all he heard was something like a little purr.

As she was falling asleep, Melanie realized Chet really was weird, but in such a good way. She could feel the warmth of his skin down the length of her body, and, for some strange reason, that was nice, too.

Chet felt Melanie's breathing more than heard it. Her hair was dry now, and he smelled the remnants of shampoo as their heads lay together on the single pillow. Then he fell asleep.

Hank and Sue Hondel went to bed but barely slept. Whatever sleep they got was fitful. Every time one or the other woke in the night, they repeated their prayers, looked out the window to see if the storm had stopped and if the sun was coming up yet. The brightening sky was at least an excuse to get out of bed. They could hear the plowing service from the Standard gas station clearing their driveway.

A few miles away, if a straight line was drawn on a map, Ellen Buçek also had been waiting for the new day. She had gotten some sleep but knew it wasn't the rest she needed.

She called down the hall to the kids' rooms. "Alex, Brad, wake up. Get outside and shovel the driveway down to the road. If the plow comes through soon enough, we're still going to church."

She heard the groggy complaints muffled under blankets but knew they would do as they were told.

Chapter 10

Melanie woke up and realized she was alone in bed. She hadn't even felt Chet leave. The room was lighter, so it must be some time in the morning, she thought. She rolled over and saw Chet near the stove. He already had the bottoms of his long underwear on and was wearing his boots.

"That's a cute ensemble."

He turned around and smiled at her. "Good morning, sleepy head."

Gigi was right about wrestlers. No wonder he was able to carry her. It wasn't a wrestling uniform, but Gigi was right about the imagination thing, too. She smirked to herself under the covers.

"Want some clothes? Some of your stuff is all dry."

He tossed her panties, long john bottoms, and the insulated long-sleeve T-shirt over to the bed.

He watched, amused and enthralled, as she ducked under the covers and came up a minute later wearing it all.

He laughed. "You remind me of a magic act I saw on *America's Got Talent* one time."

"I saw that one, too! Now for my next number..." She started going under the covers again, then came back out, grinning. "Only fooling."

They both laughed. She watched him shake out his long underwear top and pull it over his head. Magazine-ad six-pack, she noticed.

"Chet, I have to go to the bathroom," she said shyly.

"Would you like to use the upstairs restroom or the powder room on this floor?"

She knew there wasn't an upstairs but her eyes moved up toward the pointed roof anyway. "Downstairs, I guess."

He reached under the bed and pulled out a three-pound Folgers can.

"This is all this fine establishment has to offer. You can go over there in the corner, and I'll stay over here. There's a roll of TP there on the shelf."

"Don't look," she warned.

"Afraid I'll see something I haven't seen already?" he asked with a smirk.

"Be nice."

There was no disguising or muffling the noise of the urine hitting the tin can, so she started humming a song as loudly as she could. When Chet heard her scurrying back into the warm bed, he turned around.

"My turn."

She gave him his privacy by ducking under the blankets.

"Okay, I'm finished."

"Do you have any water?"

"To wash your hands?"

"No, to drink."

"I was just getting to that." He finished rearranging their shirts, socks, and sweaters on the now-empty chairs and slid them close to the stove. He shook out the jeans and hung them from the rafter above the stove. "Stay under the covers, because I have to open the door. Belle, come."

The dog bounded off the bed. Chet grabbed a big coffee pot from another shelf and went to the door with the coffee can in his other hand. He set the pot and can down on the floor, undid the latch, and slowly opened the door, trying to keep a bunch of snow from falling inside. It almost worked, until he told Belle to go out. She jumped over the drift stacked in the portal and half of it tumbled on the floor.

The world outside was covered deep in snow. The sun reflecting off the immaculate surface was blinding, forcing Chet to squint. Tree trunks and branches, coated in white, resembled a lace curtain.

Chet scraped a couple of handfuls of snow off the floor into the Folgers can, swished it around, and dumped it outside the door on the hinge side. On the latch side, he scooped freshly fallen snow into the coffee pot until it was full, packed it down with his hand, and put in some more.

All the commotion was too much for Melanie, who had her head sticking out of the covers and was holding the blankets under her chin so she could see what was going on. Chet whistled up Belle, who sprang back into the cabin in another mini-avalanche of powder. The dog shook, jangling the tags on her collar and sending a shower of melted snow onto the floor and Chet.

"Thanks, girl. It took all night to dry these out."

The snow was light enough that he was able to push the door closed without trouble.

"Are you going to make coffee?"

"Sorry, none here...."

"Good, I don't care for it anyway."

"Me, either. No, I'm going to melt some snow so we can have some water to drink."

"Why don't we just eat snow?"

"It will quench your thirst momentarily, but you can't survive on it. Your body uses up more energy melting the snow than you get from the water content."

"How do you know all this stuff?"

"I read that in one of my dad's survival manuals."

He put the big camp pot with its chipped enamel surface on top of the stove. "It won't take long. Well, let's hope we get out of here today; here goes the last of the wood and coal."

"Thank you for getting up during the night to keep the fire going."

"Had to. Can you imagine the talk at school, not to mention our folks, if they saw the headline: 'Two Naked Teens Found Dead in Frozen Embrace' and no one to tell the real story?"

Melanie laughed out loud, the best laugh he'd heard from her yet. "You crack me up," she said, laughing again. He just grinned back, happy to make her happy.

Chet poured the water into a metal cup, a part of the coffee pot set, right down to the chipped enamel, and let the water cool. She drank it all, and he poured some more.

"Is there any for you?"

"Take as much as you want. There's a lot more snow out there and the stove is still hot."

She drank another cup and handed it back. He drank a cupful and poured the rest in a saucepan that he set on the floor for Belle, who lapped it up. He put more snow on to melt, which meant opening the door again.

"Okay, I'm getting cold now, too! Let me in."

He kicked off his boots. Melanie held open the blankets for him, and he slid in beside her. The fact that it was light out and they both had clothes on changed the mood of the previous night; neither better nor worse, just different.

"So, tell me about you. You asked all the questions last time."

"Not much to tell. I grew up in town and went to school with most of the same kids since kindergarten. I've been on the soccer team four years-"

"You're good, too. I've seen you play."

"Oh yeah, when?"

"Every home game."

"For real?"

"Yep."

"I never saw you there."

"Out of those sixty thousand screaming fans, you didn't see *me?*"

She laughed. She knew when it came to drawing crowds, soccer wasn't much ahead of wrestling.

"I'd be surprised if you noticed anyone in the stands. You are so focused when you're in and I can tell you hate it when they take you out."

"You can? Yeah, it's not like cheering, which is not to say cheerleading isn't pretty demanding. I really get into soccer. I love the competition and trying to push myself. It may pay off. The University of Illinois at Chicago is starting a women's soccer program next year, and I'm being considered for a full scholarship!"

"That's great, Melanie! So, what else?"

"Been a cheerleader for two years, four-oh grade point average, including Honors English for four years. That's my life."

"I'm sure there's more than that. What about your family?"

"My dad is the local State Farm representative. Maybe you saw him on TV. After the floods here a few years ago, State Farm used him in one of the national ads for being the first agent to get insurance payouts for his clients."

"Sorry, didn't see it, but we're new here."

"Anyway, he got his degree in Business from Beloit College.

"My mom taught grade school for twenty years and decided she wanted to do something else. She retired and got her real estate license but never used it, as far as I know. My dad says she got used to staying at home. All she does now, I think, is volunteer for every rummage sale, bake sale, mission, picnic, or carnival at the church."

"What church?

"St. Anne's."

"Oh, yeah? That's where we go, too."

"My brother Jack is the oldest. Of course, his name is John, but everyone's always called him Jack. He's in pharmacy school at the University of Wisconsin, up in Madison. He just got married last summer. Next is my sister Merrily. She's in her third year at Northern Illinois over at DeKalb. Don't ask me what she wants to do; she's switched majors three times. I think the latest is Broadcast Journalism. Now she wants to be the next Laura Ingraham."

"Because she's conservative?"

"Sometimes, but mostly because she's a cancer survivor like our mom." Melanie was silent for a moment before she continued.

"Then there's me."

She gave a big, overdone smile, showing all her teeth.

"Last is my little sister Nancy, my folks' surprise child. She's nine."

"My brother Bradley is nine. He's a computer geek who likes to play video games but bummed because my folks won't let him have any games with violence in them."

"Oh, yeah? Why not?"

"You might think it's strange, with my dad being a Marine and all. He's taught us all how to shoot, but he says there's nothing fun about killing people and video games just desensitize kids to it."

"I guess I never thought about it that way. Kinda makes sense, though.

"What about sisters?"

"Just one; my sister Alexis. She's fifteen, a sophomore. She's had her own horse since she was twelve, which is fine with my folks. They figure the longer she does the horse thing, the longer it will be before she starts getting interested in boys."

"Yeah, they better be careful. She may meet someone like you." He knew from her tone she was kidding, but the tender smile that came with it said even more.

"I used to have my own horse. Sometimes I miss riding. Does your sister shoot as well as you and your brother?"

"Yes," he said, unsure if she thought that was a good thing or not.

Melanie nodded, but her expression indicated she was impressed.

"What about your folks? What do they do?"

"They met while my dad was in law school at Northwestern—"

"Your dad's a lawyer? I thought he was in the Marines."

"Yep, he is," Chet replied, puzzled at her shock. "He's a Marine lawyer. A JAG officer."

"Oh, like Colonel Sarah MacKenzie on that old TV show."

He laughed. "Yeah, sorta like that."

"That just leaves your mom."

"Like your sister, my mom switched her major in college, too. After she fell in love with Dad and knew she'd probably be moving a lot as he got transferred, she changed to Education and got a teaching credential. She'd like to teach at our school next year. We got here too late for this school year. She teaches math and geography. Alexis is hoping she doesn't get her."

"Too bad she didn't start this year. Maybe I wouldn't've had Mr. Knopp."

"Hello."

"Hello. This is Deputy Radomski from the sheriff's office. Is this Mrs. Hondel?

"Yes," she said with trepidation, unsure whether the news would bring joy or anguish.

"We promised to keep you updated on any developments. One of the pilots with the Civil Air Patrol radioed in that she spotted a small shack in the woods with smoke coming from the chimney. She says the place looks too small to be a normal residence. We think this is significant news. Most of the stranded or missing travelers from yesterday have gotten home or at least called loved ones, and this place could be within walking distance from a road leaving the Kindler place."

"Oh, Deputy! Thank you for calling! That *must* be Melanie! Hank! Come here!"

The deputy sheriff could hear talking from the partially covered phone as he waited for the woman to come back. He told himself he was going to finish his news before she could say another word.

"Do you-"

"Mrs. Hondel, one of our Search and Rescue units has already been dispatched to the area and will coordinate with some volunteers once they get there. We'll call you back if-"

"Deputy, this is Hank Hondel."

The deputy assumed Mr. Hondel had taken the phone or was listening in on an extension.

"Whereabouts is the shack located?"

"Somewhere off Laube Road where it meets Hartman is all I know right now."

"Thank you, Deputy. Please call back if you hear anything."

After getting the deputy's assurance he would keep them informed, Hank Hondel hung up. It took him less than a minute to decide his next move.

"Sue, I'm going out there."

"Are you hungry?" asked Chet.

"Starving."

"I thought I heard your stomach growl."

She looked down and gave her tummy a slap. "Is there food here, too?"

"A can of peaches."

Melanie let out another hearty chuckle.

"A cabin in the middle of the woods, and the one thing it has is peaches? How long have they been here?"

"A month or two. I brought 'em. Stay there."

Chet got up and put his boots back on. Then he retrieved a Leatherman tool from a pouch on the belt of his jeans hanging above the stove. From the shelf where he had gotten the coffee pot, he took down a large can of Del Monte sliced peaches in heavy syrup and an old metal fork. He extended the can opener on the tool, poked it through the lid, then worked it up and down around the top, until the top could be removed.

When Chet went to join Melanie, Belle was in his place getting her ears scratched.

"You've been usurped," said Melanie.

"Belle, scram." The dog went back to the end of the bed.

He sat down on the edge of the bed. Melanie sat up and put the quilt around her.

"Just one fork?"

"One bed, one cup, one fork. We weren't expecting company, huh, Belle?"

The dog looked up at the sound of her name without lifting her head off the bed.

"She's tired, and probably starving, too."

Chet speared a peach slice and held it over the can as he moved it under Melanie's chin. "One for you."

"Ymmmmmm."

"And one for me."

Back and forth they went, eating their way into the can until all the slices were gone.

"Neat, it came out even."

"Wait there."

He stood up and got the water cup.

"The can's too jagged to drink out of."

He poured the juice into the old enamel cup and handed it to her.

"This is sooo good. Here, you have some."

"No, thanks. You finish it." He watched her drain the cup, as pleased as if he'd taken her to a fine restaurant.

"Those were the best canned peaches in the whole world. For the rest of my life, whenever I have a canned peach, I don't care if it's in Jell-O, in a salad, or decoration on top of a cake, I'm going to think of these peaches."

Chet beamed. He couldn't have been prouder if he had picked and canned the peaches himself.

"So, tell me. Of all the things you could have stocked this place with, why did you bring peaches?"

"I read this story about Alaska one time..."

She emitted a little laugh and rolled her eyes. "Yes..." she urged.

"Up there, no one locks their doors and they always leave food stuffs on hand in case someone gets stranded and has to seek shelter from a blizzard. Well, in the story, all this lost guy found in the cabin was a case of canned peaches. I decided the first thing I'd put in here was that."

"You read a lot, don't you?

"So do you."

"What do you mean?"

"I'll bet you know a lot more about the clothes and furniture and carriages of Victorian England than I do."

She thought about it for a moment. "Yeah, I guess there is more in those books than just romance and sex."

They both laughed.

He tossed the can into the empty coal bucket and shook out Melanie's coat to fluff up the still-soggy feathers inside.

She slid back over so he could lie next to her again. They pulled the covers up when they started getting cold, but just lay there talking for some time, not touching each other, although their faces were no more than twelve inches apart on the one pillow. They talked about teachers, classmates, snowmen, snowball fights, places where they'd like to travel someday, and anything else that came into their minds.

"How are the clothes doing?" Melanie asked after awhile.

"The shirts were almost dry. The pants are nearly there, too. I don't think the coats will dry out until we get home."

"How *are* we going to get home?"

"We'll have to hike back to my house. It'll be as warm as it's going to get outside in a little while. You can call your folks, and I'll drive you home. My mom and sister can probably come up with some dry clothes if you want."

"How far is it?

"From here, just under three miles, I think."

"Will you carry me if I can't walk?

"Nope. You can lie down on the snow and I'll pull you by the hood of your coat like I did at the lake."

She looked at him quizzically. "When did you do that?"

"After I got you out of the water."

She looked at him like he was fooling.

"You don't remember, do you?"

"No," she said, sounding sad that she didn't.

"What do you remember?"

"I remember being scared when Tommy started groping me. I remember seeing stars after he hit me. Then I was out of the truck, running across this big field covered with snow, and I fell through the ice."

"Tommy who?"

She misunderstood the reason for his question and answered forthrightly before continuing. "Tommy Schmidt. You yelled at me in the water, so you must have been in the lake, too. Then I was trying to walk through the snow, but you carried me and I woke up here with all my clothes off."

"Were you frightened when you realized you were naked?"

"No. I was scared at first because I didn't know where I was, but then I felt safe because you were holding me and I was warm."

"You were probably going into shock from exposure or hypothermia."

"So tell me the parts I forgot."

Chet began the story from his last trap and Belle's bark and got up to the part about trying to pull her out.

"You must've had rocks in your pockets or something, because I couldn't budge you. So there you were with your arms stretched out on top of the ice, trying not to go under, and I kept telling you not to give up. Actually, you kinda reminded me of Jack holding onto the debris in *Titanic*, except I was the one on top telling you not to quit."

She hit him in the chest playfully. "I did not."

"Did too."

"Did not."

Chet gently brushed the hair from her face and cradled her cheek, the unhurt one, in his hand. She didn't take her eyes off his. As he leaned over, her head moved toward him. Their lips met, but she pulled back.

"I haven't brushed my teeth."

"You're fine; you taste like peaches."

He kissed her again. This time, she opened her mouth and he responded with his tongue. They went backwards onto the pillow, never breaking the union of their lips and mouths.

Belle started barking.

Chet's head went up. Melanie, still smiling with pleasure, waited on the pillow for him to come back. "Belle's jealous."

"No," countered Chet, "someone's coming."

He slipped on his boots as he got out of bed, and moved toward his rifle.

Chapter 11

Chet's senses became more acute. He was trying to hear what had already alerted Belle. Within seconds, he made out the distant sound of engines.

"Snowmobiles," he said.

"Oh, good. A ride home!"

"Not necessarily. Stay in bed."

Chet could tell there were at least two engines revving. He had run into plenty of snowmobilers in the past. Most were families out enjoying the winter pastime. Others were wild, cared little for the environment, and, too often, had been drinking. He kept listening and could tell the snowmobiles were getting close.

He heard a man's voice shouting to someone else but couldn't make out what was said. It would be bad enough being trapped here in his long johns by himself, but if the strangers weren't good guys, what might they do to a helpless girl who was wearing nothing but long underwear?

Chet took a step back and pulled his pants down off the rafter so he could access the sheath knife on his belt if it came to that. His parka was farther away and he didn't know if the few rounds of extra ammo he carried were too wet to fire.

He heard the first snowmobile stop outside the cabin, its engine idling. He didn't hear any of the loud talking or foul language often associated with drunks.

He decided to take the initiative by making the first move. He turned to Melanie. In an orotund whisper, he said, "Stay under the covers 'til I find out what these guys are up to."

Melanie heard the caution in Chet's voice and realized her initial glee may have been premature.

Chet opened the door. Both riders had dismounted. The tracks of one showed he had taken two steps toward the cabin. The other rider was still at the machine, but facing north toward the sound of the other snowmobile. Both men were dressed in warm hunting clothes, one with a camouflage parka and the other in fluorescent orange. Chet saw one rifle mounted on the snowmobile. From the position of the sun, he guessed it was near noon.

"'Morning, fellas," Chet said cheerfully, the door partially opened. His rifle rested on the floor, just out of view, alongside the doorjamb. "Can I help you?"

The closest guy smiled. He seemed friendly. His friend turned toward the conversation but made no move to advance. The other snowmobile was just stopping and, even through the spray of snow, looked to be pulling something.

"No," answered the man, "we thought *you* might be needin' help."

The other snowmobile, now stopped and idling, also carried two men. They were wearing some kind of long, identical parkas that reminded Chet of the Ski Patrol at a resort. He was now outnumbered by four grown men.

Chet wanted to trust them but wasn't ready to lower his guard just yet. The man shuffled through the snow a few more steps.

"What do you want here?" asked Chet, trying to put a more serious tone in his voice and casually moving the butt of the rifle-shotgun to the floor next to his foot and the barrel alongside his leg.

"Gun!" yelled one of the men on the second snowmobile, reaching into a slit pocket in his jacket and coming out with a pistol leveled at Chet. His partner was reaching for something, too, but evidently having trouble getting it out. In the distance, another snowmobile could be heard coming their direction.

"Deputy Sheriff, boy! Throw out that rifle!"

Chet was scared. He'd been around guns his whole life and knew not to be on the working end of one. But he wasn't about to be bullied because this guy didn't think he knew his rights.

Chet leaned the rifle against the wall inside the cabin again and held out both palms in front of his chest. "I have a right to a firearm in my own residence, but I set mine down. Why don't you?"

The deputy knew his bluff had been called, and he didn't want to push the situation in front of the two volunteers. He lowered his weapon but didn't reholster it. For the first time, Chet saw there was a star sewn or printed on the front of the deputies' coats.

"What's your name?"

"Chester Buçek. What's yours, sir?"

"Deputy Mike Knutson."

"May I please see your credentials, Deputy Knutson."

"Don't push it, boy," advised the other man in the same kind of parka.

"Sir, my father's a lawyer and taught me my rights. I don't have to believe you're law enforcement unless you have credentials."

Deputy Knutson turned and looked at his partner. "Can you believe this shit?" he snapped. "Watch him."

Knutson put his pistol back inside his coat, presumably reholstering it, rummaged inside somewhere else, and came out with a wallet that he flipped open. One side held a six-pointed star badge, and the other side, a card that resembled a photo ID, as best as Chet could tell from the distance.

"Satisfied?" Knutson growled.

"Yes, sir. Thank you."

"We're looking for a missing girl. Name's Melanie Hondel. You seen her?"

"Yes, sir. She's inside. Will you be able to take her home?"

The other snowmobile was drawing near, and everyone turned a moment to see who was coming.

"Yeah, kid. We're going to take her home." Both deputies were already moving toward the cabin.

Chet turned his head to look inside the cabin. "Melanie! It's the sheriff, here to take you home!"

"Great!" said Melanie, her head coming out from under the covers just in time to see what happened next.

As soon as Chet turned, the deputies hurried as best they could through the snow and before he turned back, they grabbed him, swung him around, and slammed his face and body into the door.

The second deputy pressed his entire body against Chet, squashing him into the rough, frost-covered wood, and whispered over Chet's shoulder, "So your dad's a lawyer, huh?"

Even though Chet was wearing only long underwear and his rubber hiking boots, one of them roughly patted him down for additional weapons, pressing his testicles until he winced.

"Now just stand there, don't move, and don't say a word," the deputy ordered.

Deputy Knutson snatched Chet's rifle, opened the breach, and removed both live rounds. He began to move further into the cabin only to be confronted by Belle, who was standing on the bed over Melanie, growling.

The deputy assumed the dog belonged to Chet. "Control this dog, kid, or we may have to shoot it for being vicious."

"Belle!" As soon as he knew he had her attention, Chet said, "Down," moving his open hand, palm down, toward the floor. The pointer obeyed but continued to stay alert for her master's next command.

"Are you Melanie Hondel?" asked Deputy Knutson.

"Yes."

"Good. Get dressed. We're taking you outta here."

The other two men stayed outside, watching everything as the other snowmobile pulled up.

"Where's your clothes, kid?" asked the deputy holding Chet.

"Over there."

"Put 'em on."

"Yes, sir," answered Chet, wiping the blood dripping from his nose with the back of his hand.

Melanie felt embarrassed getting out of bed with just her underwear on within view of four strange men, and was very slowly pulling back the covers when her father appeared in the doorway.

"Daddy!" she yelled.

"Melanie! Are you okay?"

The look of elation on his face changed to something between shame and disgust when he saw her get out of bed wearing just the tops and bottoms of snug long underwear, her developing woman's body quite evident beneath it.

Hank Hondel saw the deputies ogling his daughter as she stretched to reach her jeans hanging above the potbellied stove and began to put them on. His attempt to approach her was blocked by the deputy dealing with a young man and the hot stove.

To get the men's attention, Hank Hondel said, "Deputies, thank you so much for finding my daughter."

"Our pleasure, sir. We found her here with this guy," said Deputy Knutson, jutting his Jay Leno chin toward Chet, who was pulling on his jeans.

"I'll take that knife, kid," Knutson's partner said to Chet, who drew it from its sheath and handed it to him, grip first.

Deputy Knutson addressed Melanie. "Melanie, we're going to put you in what we call a 'mummy bag.' It's like a large sleeping bag. It'll keep you warm and dry so we can pull you out on our sled."

"Okay," said Melanie, resigned to the fact that things were out of her control. "Will Chet come with us?"

"Oh, yeah. We'll squeeze him in."

Chet caught Melanie's eye and moved his gaze toward Belle. "Deputy, could my dog ride with me?" she asked.

Melanie's father whipped a nasty look at her but remained silent.

"Sure, Melanie," said Knutson's partner. "Okay, fellas, bring the mummy bag."

The volunteers entered carrying the thick but lightweight bag, insulated for subzero temperatures.

Mr. Hondel, a tall, slightly overweight man, older than the others, looked contemptuously at Chet, who was now putting on his socks and boots, as he followed the men toward Melanie. Melanie was being zipped into the bag when she saw her father approaching, and looked up to smile at him. For the first time, he saw her face close-up.

"What happened to you?"

"I got hit..."

Hank Hondel spun around, quickly covered the short distance to Chet, and grabbed him with both hands around the throat, squeezing. Shocked at first, Chet grabbed the man's wrists and tried to pull them free. He started to gag.

"You hit my daughter? You dared to hit my daughter?" he yelled. He let go with his right hand and cocked it back to punch Chet, when both deputies grabbed him and pulled him backwards.

"Daddy!" screamed Melanie. "Leave him alone! He saved my life!"

"Don't do it, Mr. Hondel. Assaulting a minor can get you in big trouble," one of them warned him.

"I want him arrested!"

Chet tried to protest. "I didn't do-"

"Did I tell you to keep your mouth shut?" bellowed the second deputy.

Hank Hondel turned to Melanie. "Did he touch you?"

"No, Daddy."

Melanie wanted to move toward Chet, but even if she hadn't been confined in the mummy bag, her father was blocking her path in the small cabin.

"Did you sleep together?"

"Well, sort of, but not like *that*," she answered, knowing what her father was implying.

"Did he bring you here and keep you here overnight?"

"He brought me...carried me...here, but didn't 'keep' me here. He saved-"

Hank Hondel turned back to the deputies, his face red. "I want him arrested! For kidnapping, false imprisonment, assault and battery, and attempted rape!"

Melanie screamed her objections, trying to explain, but no one paid attention to her.

Deputy Knutson looked at Melanie's swollen, cut lip and bruised face.

"We can't arrest him on the battery because it's a misdemeanor not committed in our presence. But because she's a minor, you can make a citizen's arrest."

"Then that's what I want to do!"

Melanie was crying, still screaming, "No, no, you can't do that!"

"Okay, guys, go ahead and load her up."

The volunteers each put an arm behind Melanie's thighs and another behind her back, lifting her into a sitting position as they carried her out to the sled.

"We'll need you to sign some paperwork when we get back to our car, but I still need to take a statement from her. Our report will go to detectives who'll decide what other charges are appropriate."

"She's too hysterical and traumatized to be interviewed now. Have your detectives talk to her at home tomorrow."

Knutson's partner chimed in, "If they're boyfriend and girlfriend, maybe a domestic violence charge would fly, too."

Chet listened to the exchange and rubbed his throat but decided neither Melanie's father nor the deputies were going to listen to anything he had to say.

The three snowmobiles followed their tracks back to the road. A white van with a satellite on top and bearing the logo of one of the Rockford television stations was now parked with the vehicles of the sheriff, Hank Hudson, and the two volunteers who had brought out their snowmobile. Like much of the news media, they probably monitored the police radio band and had heard the report of the possible rescue.

As her father loaded the family's snowmobile, Melanie was removed from the mummy bag by the volunteers. A reporter and her cameraman came dashing over, film running.

"Is this the girl who was reported missing yesterday?"

Without waiting for an answer, the reporter shoved a microphone in Melanie's face and rattled off questions, hoping Melanie would bite on one of them.

"Are you okay? How did you get those injuries on your face? Where did you spend the night? How did you get lost?"

Melanie looked to her dad for support, but when none seemed forthcoming, she just shook her head no, without answering any questions. When Melanie got into her father's SUV with a reluctant Belle, the film crew approached Hank Hondel.

"Good afternoon, sir. What's your name? Is that your daughter? How does it feel to have your daughter back?" Hank snapped, "No comment," to each question and got in his SUV and drove off. The cameraman said something to the reporter and their focus changed to Chet and the sheriff's deputies. They filmed some footage of Chet being taken off a snowmobile and getting handcuffed.

The news crew hustled over toward the law enforcement vehicle. The reporter slipped on the icy road and would have fallen, except her cameraman caught her. Chet stood on the side of the road, shivering, while he waited for the snowmobiles to be loaded on their trailers.

The reporter walked right up to Deputy Knutson so she could read the name tag sewn on the outside of his winter coat. "Good afternoon, Deputy Knutson, were you and the other deputy instrumental in rescuing that young woman today?"

"Yes. Us and these volunteers," he said, pointing to the other men.

"Do you know where the young woman spent the night?"

Knutson wasn't sure if investigators might want to bring evidence technicians out to the cabin, and fearing possible destruction or theft of evidence, he decided not to reveal that information.

"Yes, she found a place to get out of the wind for the night."

"Is that man under arrest?"

"Yes, he's in custody pending further investigation."

"What has he been charged with?"

"Nothing yet. Charging will be up to the State's Attorney. He was arrested for battery and is being held for possible sexual assault."

"Rape?" asked the reporter.

"I'd rather not speculate at this point," Deputy Knutson said, but the look on his face gave the reporter the answer she wanted.

"Is there...?"

"I'm sorry; we really have to get going."

After thanking the volunteers for their help, the deputies put Chet in the backseat of their Chevy Suburban with sheriff's insignias on the sides. Chet saw the cameraman still filming the vehicle as it pulled away.

It was midafternoon when they arrived at the sheriff's substation for that section of the county. The deputies removed the handcuffs and Chet was allowed to use the bathroom and get a drink from a water fountain. Before he could fully quench his thirst, he was forced to move. They placed him in a small holding cell by himself until transportation could be arranged to juvenile hall.

The cell had no outside window and the bar door faced a blank wall of a hallway. Chet could hear people talking, occasional voices coming over police radios, and someone pecking on a keyboard. He sat on the metal-framed bed with its legs bolted to the floor and wondered when he might get fed and what would happen next. He also thought about Melanie. He felt so lucky that it was he who had saved her, and that she seemed to be the type of person he had always imagined her to be. He thought she may like him a little, too, but didn't know if that would change now that the emergency was over. It angered him that her father thought he was the one who hit her.

It seemed some time before anyone came down the hall, but an older deputy with a protruding stomach, white hair, and white moustache passed by.

Chet hurried to the bars. "Can I have another drink of water?"

"Sure," the deputy replied in a kindly voice. He returned a minute later and handed Chet a bottle of Aquafina through the door. "Here you go."

"Thank you. Do you know if I'll get something to eat pretty soon?"

"No meals are served here, but I suspect they'll feed you as soon as you get to the hall. I'd get you something to tide you over, but our candy machine is broken."

"Well, thanks anyway, and thank you again for the water."

"Don't mention it," the old deputy said with a smile before heading down the short hall and out of sight.

The sun had already set by the time Chet was turned over to a female deputy whom he overhead would deliver him to "kiddie jail."

"We'll write our reports in the morning and have them ready for the dicks when they come in Monday," he heard Deputy Knutson tell the new deputy, a husky woman with her hair in a French braid.

The female deputy pushed Chet's coat through the bars in the door and told him to put it on, then to face the wall. After he did, she unlocked the cell, came in, and put him back in handcuffs.

All her orders were short and brusque, except for one comment, more to herself, as she led him out to the parking lot. "You mean they didn't take your shoelaces away from you?"

She buckled him in the back of a squad car. A metal mesh screen separated the back seat from the front. Though she didn't smoke in the car, Chet could smell tobacco smoke on her clothes. The deputy didn't say a word during the entire trip to the county juvenile detention facility along the Rock River on the north side of Rockford. The silence was broken only when the sheriff's dispatcher could be heard on the radio transmitting information to deputies in other cars and when they responded. Most of the main roads had been plowed but ice had formed, so it took them over an hour of slow driving.

The parking area at the facility's intake entrance had not been plowed; arriving and departing law enforcement vehicles had compressed the surface to arctic-quality hard pack. The snow made crunching sounds as the big Crown Victoria drove over it. Once the car was parked, the deputy opened the back door and motioned to Chet, speaking for the first time since they'd left the substation.

"Out."

The detention officer, a small Hispanic woman with heavy eye makeup and strong perfume, stood up from her desk behind the intake counter and spoke to the deputy. Chet didn't pay attention to what was said until the deputy sheriff pulled a goldenrod sheet of paper from a rack containing a variety of multi-colored forms.

"Name."

Chet stated his full name and told her how to write his last name. She gave him a dirty look and wrote the standard English letters.

"Date of birth."

Chet gave her the month, date, and year.

"Home address."

As Chet began to answer, the intake officer looked up from whatever she was working on.

"He's eighteen. He doesn't come here."

The deputy looked at the DOB and computed the age.

"Damn, he just turned eighteen."

"Two weeks ago," agreed Chet.

"You'll have to take him to the central jail," said the intake officer.

"Ain't happenin' tonight," the deputy proclaimed. "I just worked a double shift because of the storm and I come back on in the morning. I need some sleep. You'll have to find a place to keep him tonight. I'll call dispatch and have someone transport him in the morning."

The intake officer moaned and whined about policies, but the deputy wasn't having any of it. Irritated that something so simple was being turned into a major issue, the deputy tossed the officer the completed booking sheet and the citizen's arrest form with notes that the arrest was being referred to Investigations for the rape and other charges. Then she roughly took the cuffs off Chet, returned them to the handcuff case on her gun belt, and left, forgetting that Deputy Knutson had asked her to contact the boy's parents.

The intake deputy gave Chet a dirty look as she spoke on the phone to some superior, then looked up. "Adults cannot be housed with juveniles. That's the rule. You'll have to be in a cell by yourself until they come for you."

In response, Chet shrugged in surrender, wondering what say he would have had in the matter, in any event.

The officer moved Chet from the booking area into the next room with carts and shelves full of clothes and supplies. She handed him a cotton jumpsuit, a pair of cheap flip-flops, and a plastic bag with a few toiletries in it. She then led him through a series of doors and metal gates. Chet could hear lots of boys talking and laughing in the cell blocks they passed. When they got to an empty cell in a deserted block, the officer unlocked it with a wide brass key and told Chet to take off all his clothes except his underwear and put on the jumpsuit.

"Will I get anything to eat?"

"You missed the evening meal," she said in a tone that implied it was Chet's fault he was late. "There'll be a bedtime snack in an hour or so."

As instructed, Chet put his clothes in a big paper shopping bag the officer had brought along and which she took with her when she left, warning him not to cause any trouble.

Chet brushed his teeth and washed his hands and face in the stainless steel sink. The sink had a tiny water fountain from which he was able to quench his thirst.

Terrible hunger pains gnawed at his insides. He recognized the headache that was forming when he went too long without eating. Throughout wrestling season, he maintained a strict limit on his food intake so he could always qualify for his class at weigh-in.

He computed back and realized he had missed two dinners, a breakfast, and a lunch. The hunger pains seemed to dissipate a little when he thought about sharing his last meal - a snack, really - with Melanie and how she had said she would always remember the canned peaches. The memory of it made him smile.

He guessed the county didn't want any of their juvenile charges getting a chill, because they weren't stingy with the heat. He was uncomfortably warm, so he took off his long underwear and put the jumpsuit back on.

Around nine p.m., a guard came around with a cart loaded with ice cream sandwiches. *Now there's a treat for a cold winter's night,* thought Chet, who was still happy to get it. Better, when he told the guard he had arrived after the evening meal, the guard tossed him another one. In six bites, both sandwiches were gone.

Chet brushed his teeth again and got into the bottom bunk even before a man's voice came over a public address system announcing, "Fifteen minutes until lights out." He mumbled some prayers, wondered if Melanie had fed Belle, then, exhausted, he fell to sleep.

Chapter 12

Slick spots developed on the plowed roads as Melanie and her father drove home, slowing their progress. Neither spoke for some time until Melanie broke the silence. "I can't believe you attacked him, Daddy."

"I can't believe you were out here sleeping with him while your mother and I were worried sick all night."

"What is it? That you can't believe I slept with him or you can't believe I didn't have sex with him?"

Hank Hondel was angry with himself more than with his daughter, but he was not about to be drawn into an argument with a tired, emotional seventeen-year-old.

When her father refused to respond, Melanie went on without him. "Do you understand, I fell through the ice? Chet saved me. We were both soaking wet and freezing, we couldn't stay in the wet clothes, and the only warm place was under the blankets."

"You mean you didn't have your underwear on all night?" asked Hank, picturing her in what she was wearing when he arrived.

"Of course not. I just told you, everything was totally soaked. Chet wrung out what he could and hung our clothes by the stove to dry."

"I hope you're proud of yourself."

"What's that supposed to mean?" she said with a tone that was both sarcastic and nasty. "I have *nothing* to be ashamed of."

"Watch your tone, young lady."

"Or what?"

"You're not too old to get a lickin'." Hank felt foolish as soon as he said that. He had never spanked Melanie in her life and certainly wouldn't do it now.

"Ha! I'd like to see you try."

Icy silence descended for the remainder of the drive.

When they got home, Melanie jumped out with Belle as soon as the car stopped to wait for the garage door to open. She went into the house, removed her boots in the back hall, and continued on to the kitchen.

"Melanie! You're home!" exclaimed her mother, rushing into the kitchen.

Melanie let her mother hug her and returned it half-heartedly.

"What happened to your face?" her mother asked.

"I got hit. Where's Molly?" asked Melanie, speaking of the family's half cocker spaniel-half dachshund.

"I suppose she's upstairs with Nancy. What do you mean you got hit? Who hit you?"

Melanie ignored her mother's question and retrieved two saucepans from the cupboard. "Please ask her to keep Molly up there. I'll keep Belle in my room." Melanie opened the refrigerator and removed a half-empty five-pound bag of dry dog food and poured some into one of the pans.

After a worry-filled, sleepless night, Melanie's lack of respect more than her reticence irritated Sue Hondel. "Well, I'd like to know where you were last night and why you never called." She turned at the sound of her husband coming in, seeing at the same time the terrible scowl Melanie gave him.

"Is someone going to tell me what happened?" Sue asked them both.

"Just tell your judgmental husband that I'm a virgin today and I'll be a virgin on my wedding night," snarled Melanie.

WHACK!

Melanie's head rocked sideways, her body following a split-second later. Some of the kibble spilled out of the pan, which Belle quickly gobbled up. Only then did Melanie begin to feel the sting on her cheek where her mother had just slapped her.

"Who do you think you're talking to?"

Melanie started crying and ran to her room, followed by Belle wanting more of the dog food.

When the reality of what she had just done dawned on her, Sue started to cry, too. Hank took her in his arms.

"What happened out there?" she asked. "And where did the dog come from?"

Alexis Buçek was at the family computer in the dining room, typing a report on ancient Egypt when the phone rang. She and her father exchanged cheery greetings, but she could tell he was speaking in his shorthand business voice.

"Mom! It's Dad!" Alexis yelled.

Ellen, who was preparing for bed, grabbed the extension in the master bedroom upstairs.

"Hi, Peter! Where are you?"

"Just landed at Andrews. Got hung up in Germany due to foul weather. While we were on the ground, I called a buddy of mine over at the Navy-Marine Appellate Court in D.C. He had his wife get me a reservation on the first commercial flight out of Reagan National to O'Hare in the morning and held it with his own AmEx. I'll be staying at their place tonight.

"Chet home yet?"

"No. I couldn't wait for you to reach the States. I called the sheriff just after noon to report him missing."

"That's fine, honey. More eyes can't hurt."

"They told me they've had numerous calls. A lot of people got stranded in the storm and just haven't made it home yet."

"I'm sure that's what happened to Chet. He'll be fine; you'll see."

"How long will it take to get here?"

"It takes as long to fly to O'Hare as it will take me to drive from there to home. If I make that first flight, five hours at the very best, probably closer to six."

"Drive safely, Peter. But hurry."

Melanie was in that half-sleep just before coming awake but realized she was too warm. She opened her eyes and recognized her own bedroom. It took her a moment to remember what had happened and the last thing she recalled was lying on her bed, crying.

She lifted her head off the pillow and rolled sideways, discovering she had on all of her clothes. *No wonder I'm warm.* She licked her lips a few times to get some moisture in her dry mouth, then was startled when she felt the bed move. She rolled over and saw Belle.

She laughed. "No wonder I'm warm!" she said. She tussled the dog's head. "Got used to sleeping in bed with me, huh, girl?"

Her thoughts immediately returned to Chet and the time they had spent together. It felt like she'd been in an adventure with a brave hero, except it had all been real. She wondered what the sheriffs had done with him, if he was home yet, and what he was doing at that very moment. She thought of calling him but remembered her cell phone was broken. She wasn't about to go in her parents' room or to the kitchen and use the family phone.

She lay there for a few more minutes, stretched, and got up, ready to take a shower. She crossed her arms in front of her and pulled the sweater over her head. About to repeat the motion for the long-sleeve, insulated T-shirt, her eyes stopped in the corner of the room.

She strode over to the huge stuffed panda and her other prize from the fair. She yanked the plastic lei off the bear's neck, ripped it to shreds, and threw the pieces in the waste-basket. She looked down at the remnants. *Tommy should be the one in jail.* "Jerk. I hope I never see him again."

She finished undressing, got halfway to the bathroom, and went back to the stuffed bear. She picked it up and hugged it. *I hope Chet's okay. Why didn't I go out with him last fall?*

With the 10 p.m.-to-8 a.m. graveyard shift nearly over, the probation officer on the intake desk at the juvenile detention facility was clearing the desk and double-checking his work before he went off duty. He picked up the paperwork on that eighteen-year-old prisoner Officer Sanchez had told him about before she had gone home last night. *Poor kid*, thought the probation officer, *missed being handled by the juvenile court by only two weeks.* Suddenly, his eyes bugged out and his blood pressure went up. The boxes on the intake form showing the name of the parent or guardian who was notified about the status of the detainee, as well as the time the call was placed, were blank!

"Why am I getting stuck with this?" he asked himself out loud.

He picked up the phone and punched in the number provided by the detainee.

"Hello."

"This is Detention Officer Brown at the Winnebago County Juvenile Detention Center. Is Mr. or Mrs. Bucek there?"

"This is Ellen Buçek."

"Mrs. Bucek," he started, still mispronouncing the name, "I apologize for this late notice. Somehow this matter slipped through the cracks last night. I can assure you it was completely inadvertent, but we have your son. Chester is fine, but in custody down here. We can release him to you or Mr. Bucek if you wish to come and get him."

"Of course," said Ellen, irritated that she had worried all night for nothing, curious why he was at juvenile hall, but still relieved Chet was safe. "I'll get there as quickly as I can." She listened as the officer gave her directions and where to go upon her arrival.

Officer Brown hung up, pleased the mother wasn't as upset as he'd feared she would be. He looked up and saw one of his fellow officers enter the room.

"Kevin, you're just in time. I've got to use the head before I clock out. Would you cover the desk for a few minutes until the next shift comes on? I gotta go bad."

"Sure, Darrin, go ahead."

Damn, thought Officer Kevin Maxwell as he sat down behind the desk, *no good turn goes unpunished*. No sooner had Darrin left for the bathroom when he saw a sheriff's car pulling up in the parking lot outside their door. *Hmm, what's this? No kid?*

"Good morning, Deputy. Bringing us a live one?"

"No, actually, I'm here to take one off your hands. Dispatch sent me here to pick up some eighteen-year-old you kept overnight for us."

Officer Maxwell scanned the desk and saw the paperwork front and center. Bingo!

"Here it is. Chester Bucek. Just sign this release form and you can have him."

The studded snow tires hummed on the plowed roads. The deputy was wearing a thick insulated nylon jacket and a hat with furry earflaps turned up on the sides. Even though it was below freezing, he was driving with his window halfway down and the heat on full blast. Chet was getting cold because his coat was still damp and not holding in his body heat very well. Rolling it up and stuffing it in a paper bag the previous night hadn't helped dry it out.

"Pretty serious charges, kid."

"I didn't do anything wrong."

"Uh huh."

They continued on for a few minutes, when the deputy asked, "How old'ja tell 'em ya were."

"Eighteen."

"Is that how old ya really are?"

"Yes, sir."

"Ya sure you're not seventeen?"

"I'm sure."

"Look, kid, tell me ya lied back there and you're really seventeen and I can take ya back to juvenile hall. By the time they figure out you're an adult, they may have that trouble back there worked out."

"I didn't lie. I'm really eighteen."

"Kid, you're too honest for your own good. Ya'ver been in jail before?"

What kind of guy does he think I am? wondered Chet.

"No, sir."

"Listen up and pay attention to what I'm gonna tell ya. Ya probably won't be in there long cuz your folks will bail ya out.

Don't be friends with anyone, even if they try to be friends with you. Answer polite if any of the other prisoners talk to ya, but don't get in any long conversations. Don't sit on any benches; some guy will say you're sittin' in his spot just to throw his weight around. Sit on the floor against a wall and keep your eyes open. In fact, except when the deputies are movin' ya, try to keep your back to the wall as much as possible. And don't stare at anyone; it's a sure way to invite a fight. If there is a fight, don't get involved; get yourself away and your back against a wall. Ya got all that?"

"Yes, sir. Thank you."

"Melanie, are you coming down for breakfast?"

"No. I don't feel well. Maybe I'll eat later."

"Are you well enough to go to school? You can ride in with Dad if you want."

"Yes, I'm going to school. And I'll take the bus."

"She hasn't come down from her room except to take that dog out since you brought her home," Sue Hondel said to her husband, who was putting on his hat and coat to leave for work.

"Maybe she's eating dog food."

"Oh, Hank. Be serious. I'm concerned."

"Honey, she's not going to starve. She either had snacks stashed up there, she's sneaking down when we're not around, or Nancy's smuggling her food."

"I am not," retorted Nancy, offended at being considered a culprit.

As soon as she heard her father pull his car from the garage, Melanie came down.

Chapter 13

Randy Roark put down the morning paper, picked up the phone, and called his secretary. "Martha, who's Jail Commander right now?"

There was a brief delay while she checked.

"Ben Herrera."

He knew the number by heart and punched it in.

"Commander's Office, Deputy Ferguson."

"Ferguson, this is the sheriff." He could almost hear the inhalation of fear-filled breath on the other end. He smirked. He considered it one of the perks of his position. "Is Captain Herrera there?"

"Right here, sir. Please hold on." The guy was trying to muffle the receiver, but he heard every word. "Captain! It's the sheriff!"

Post haste, the phone was answered.

"Yes, sir, how can I help you?"

"You got a kid down there named Chester Buçek?" He pronounced it "Boo-sek."

"Let me check my in-custody roster. Yep, Chester Bucek, white male adult. Arrived early this morning. He just finished processing and was moved to a holding cell pending assignment to a block."

"Put him back in his own clothes and bring him up here with his property."

It was not usual procedure, so the hesitation didn't surprise Roark, but he had to remind them who was in charge.

"Captain, did I say something you didn't understand?"

"Uh, no, sir. Did you mean your office?"

"When I say 'up here,' what did you think I meant? The employee cafeteria?"

"No, sir! I'll have the prisoner escorted to your office forthwith!"

"Thank you, Captain. By the way, how's Yesenia doing?"

Roark could hear the surprise in the captain's voice. *What a boss, he's thinking, he even remembers the name of my wife! God, I love this job,* thought Roark.

"Real well, sir. Thank you. I'll tell her you asked."

"And what about Andrea? She doing well in college? This is her first year, right?"

"Yes, sir. She's fine, too. We expected better grades but her counselor said there's often an adjustment between high school and college."

"I'm sure she'll surprise you this semester. Thank you, Captain." Before the commander could say "good-bye," Roark hung up.

Chet was sitting on the floor against a wall like the deputy had told him, happy to have received the advice. He realized it was an eye-opening experience he never wanted to repeat; he found the whole ordeal humiliating. Worse than that, he was afraid. He had always felt confident in his ability to take care of himself, but he'd never anticipated a situation like this.

Simply knowing these men, all older than him, had been arrested for some crime was scary enough. But he could tell most of them were tough with either little or extreme emotions, and the muscles on many were a sign of likely physical strength. He was old enough and well-traveled enough to know these men did not operate under the same moral code he did. They obviously had been arrested for hurting someone or taking something that didn't belong to them. Still, he had been treated just like these other prisoners since he got there.

After he had been searched, fingerprinted, and photographed, he was ordered to walk single-file with other prisoners to another room with benches. There, he had been forced to strip and put all his clothes in a large, clear plastic bag. Everyone had to bend over and spread their butt cheeks while a jailer with rubber gloves and wearing a mask over his nose and mouth walked down the line and examined them for secreted contraband.

Then it was on to a large shower room with shower heads up high where they couldn't be reached. They had been told to use the soap from the dispensers on the wall and not to forget to wash their hair. The soap smelled like Lysol. As the prisoners left the shower area, a deputy handed each one a thin towel, a size somewhere between a hand towel and a bath towel, barely adequate for drying.

An inmate wearing tan clothes, called a trustee, had a big cart with jail uniforms stacked on it. He looked at each person and decided what size they should get. Chet was handed size large boxer shorts and orange jumpsuit. The uniform fit okay but the underwear was too big and kept falling down, reinforcing Chet's judgment that briefs were best.

From there, the men were moved to a big cell with lots of other prisoners. Chet listened to other guys who had evidently been here before and learned that the deputies were deciding to which block of the jail each prisoner would be assigned and with whom they would bunk. It seemed the type of crime, gang affiliation, special medical needs, and sexual orientation were some of the considerations.

Chet wasn't the smallest guy in the sorting cell, but he was the youngest. He saw a lot of the older guys looking at him. He did like he'd been told, staying aware, but not staring at anyone.

A dozen or so prisoners were called by name, went to the gate, were handcuffed and taken away.

A guy walked up, looked down at Chet, and asked him what he was in for.

"I didn't do anything."

The guy snorted. "Kid, none of us did it. What charges did they book you on?"

"They told me kidnapping, false imprisonment, and rape."

The guy gave him a disgusted look and walked away.

"Boo-sek!" yelled the uniformed deputy at the gate.

Chet stood up and walked quickly to the deputy.

"Hands out to your sides."

He did so and the deputy locked a chain around his waist, then secured his wrists to handcuffs attached to the chain. No one else who had left had been cuffed like this, but Chet just followed orders. He noticed everyone in the cell was watching him. He heard the guy who spoke to him telling some others, "Rape." The other prisoners scowled, and one Hispanic guy turned sideways and spit on the cell floor in contempt.

They walked back the way Chet had been brought in. The deputy stopped at a counter along the way and picked up his bag of clothes that another deputy had waiting. Around the corner was the initial intake room that was empty at the moment. The deputy took off the handcuffs and waist chain, then told him to remove the jail clothes and put his own back on. When he was dressed, the chain and cuffs were replaced.

They got on an elevator. The deputy made him stand in the corner facing the wall and kept his hand on the waist chain at the small of Chet's back. When the doors opened, they were in a long office. Chet could hear keyboards clacking, copy machines humming, and announcements on an overhead PA. Secretaries, some cute and some dowdy, worked at desks or walked around carrying papers or files.

They stopped at a door of frosted glass painted with the words

RANDALL R. ROARK
SHERIFF
WINNEBAGO COUNTY

in black under a picture of a sheriff's badge. The deputy knocked twice on the wood frame, and a loud voice inside bellowed, "Enter."

Behind the desk sat a burly man, of medium height but solidly built like an NFL lineman, wide chest, shoulders like a bull, and no visible neck. He looked up, and the deputy said, "Deputy Ferguson reporting with prisoner Boo-sek, sir."

"Remove the cuffs and waist chain."

The deputy looked at the sheriff as if to say, "Are you sure?" The sheriff was just opening his mouth to say something when the deputy blurted, "Right away, sir."

When the restraints were removed, the sheriff said, "Thank you, Deputy Ferguson. You may go back to your duties. I can handle this."

"Yes, sir." The deputy shut the door behind him.

"Have a seat."

Chet moved to sit on a chair near the door, but the man motioned him to one of the two leather-covered chairs with brass upholstery tacks positioned in front of the big mahogany desk.

"So you're the notorious Chester Boo-sek I saw on TV earlier today?"

"It's pronounced Bew-check, sir."

The sheriff wasn't used to being corrected, particularly by prisoners. Especially by prisoners to whom he'd already shown a kindness, but right was right.

"Sorry. Buçek."

"I don't know about the notorious part, but, yes, I'm Chester Buçek."

"Is your father Peter Buçek? Lieutenant Colonel Peter Buçek, United States Marine Corps?"

With pride in his voice, Chet said he was.

"I had my TV on..." The sheriff motioned to a flat screen television mounted on the wall, presently muted. "And I see this news coverage about my deputies up north arresting some teenager for terrible crimes against a pretty young high school girl. Then, while I'm sitting here finally getting around to reading the *Register Star*, I see this article titled, 'Area Marine Awarded Bronze Star.'

"I haven't worked Investigations in quite a while, but I was able to deduce that a man and a boy being from the same small town with the same last name might happen to be related."

He smiled at his own joke. Chet just nodded affirmatively.

"Have you called anyone yet?"

"No."

"Why not?"

"When they took us to the phones, some other guy pushed me away so he could use it even though it was my turn. The deputy who drove me here told me not to get in trouble with the other prisoners, so I just let him have it. Then the jailer came back and said our time was up."

"You want to call a lawyer?"

"I don't have one." *Except my dad,* he thought.

"Call your mother and tell her to come get you."

The sheriff turned the phone around on his desk and handed the receiver to Chet. "Make your call, but since there's no recorder on this phone, I have to listen in. Dial nine for an outside line."

Chet nodded okay as he dialed home. When he was finished, the sheriff pressed the Speaker button on the unit.

"Hello."

"Brad, it's Chet. Is Mom there"?

"No, she went to juvenile hall to get you."

"Brad, listen. Tell Mom I'm in *the* sheriff's office in Rockford. Ask her to come here and then I can go home. You got all that?"

"Sure, Chet." The nine-year-old repeated the instructions almost verbatim.

"Okay, great. Try to get her on her cell phone. Otherwise, be sure to tell her as soon as she comes home or if she calls home first."

"Okay, I will."

"'Bye, Brad.

"'Bye, Chet," he said, melancholy in his voice.

"You want anything to eat?" asked the sheriff.

"No, thank you. I'm fine."

"Boy, when was the last time you ate and what was it?"

"Half a can of peaches yesterday morning and two ice cream sandwiches last night."

The sheriff shook his head. "I'm not even going to ask." He turned his phone back around and hit a key on the speed dial.

"Martha, call the cafeteria. Tell them to send that soup, sandwich and fries thing to my office. Tell them I want it hot and I want it five minutes ago." Pause. "I don't know, hold on."

"You want coffee, soda, milk, what?"

"Can I have water?"

"Two bottles of water." Pause. "Yes, tell them to put it on my personal account. Thank you, Martha."

While they waited for the food to be delivered, the sheriff studied his prisoner's face a moment, then asked, "Did you do the stuff you're charged with?"

"No, sir."

"Make me believe you."

"How? All I can tell you is I was attracted to Melanie right from the start of the year, when I transferred to that school. Yes, she's pretty, but she's kind, and smart, and fun, too. But I don't care who she was, I would never do those things to any girl."

"Did the inmates find out what you were in for?"

"Yes, sir."

"How did they react when they found out?"

"They acted disgusted, and one guy even spit on the floor."

"Rapists aren't treated well in the jail, even worse in prison."

"How come?"

"Even crooks have wives, girlfriends, mothers, daughters, sisters. They don't want to imagine anything like that happening to their women while they're inside."

The food arrived. The sheriff turned around and went to work on his computer and making phone calls while Chet wolfed down the food with the best manners he could muster. When he was done, Chet wiped his mouth with the paper napkin and thanked the sheriff for the meal.

"Sir, can I ask why I'm up here."

"Kid, the law may consider you an adult, but you'd be mincemeat if you stayed in that place for long. Knowing who your dad is, I don't figure you're much of a flight risk. You'll be better off at home. I know some kids go sideways or act out when their dads are away, so maybe that's what happened here."

"I told you, I didn't do anything."

"Uh huh. Well, while we wait for your mother, why don't you tell me exactly what happened. And don't leave anything out!"

Chet started the story with him and Belle out on his trap line and finished it with the arrival of the search team. He only omitted the personal stuff about Melanie and the part about the deputies roughing him up and Melanie's dad choking him.

The sheriff had been leaning back in his black leather chair with his hands behind his head, listening intently for any hint of prevarication or exaggeration.

"Damn, boy. How'd you end up here? They ought to be giving you a parade. You're a hero."

Chet blushed at the compliment, still bewildered about the entire turn of events. His eyes dropped to the remaining half bottle of water in his hands. When he looked up, the sheriff was still looking at him.

"You love her, don't you?"

Chet nodded. "If there's any justice in the world, I'm going to marry that girl someday."

The sheriff nodded his head in agreement.

His phone buzzed.

"Yes, Martha? Send her right in."

The sheriff was already coming around his desk when Chet's mother was shown in by the secretary.

Ellen Buçek saw her son as soon as she got past the door and wrapped him a hug that Chet, somewhat embarrassed by display of emotion, returned. Still holding her son's arms, Ellen then stepped back to examine him for any sign of trauma before turning toward the man she assumed was the sheriff.

"Mrs. Buçek, it's a real pleasure to meet you." They shook hands.

From the time she had arrived at the building, Ellen had been surprised and impressed at the civility and assistance she'd been provided. It was like they'd been waiting for her to get there. She had barely removed the long wool scarf from her head before she was being escorted by a sergeant to the sheriff's office. Equally surprising was the immediate greeting from the man himself, who she saw was only slightly taller than she was but as thick as a mailbox on a downtown street corner.

"I've just been sitting here chatting with your son. Seems like a fine young man. I'm sorry Chester had to go through all that rigmarole downstairs, but he wasn't there long. I don't know all what's going on with this case, but I'm going to look into it personally."

"Thank you, Mr. Roark. That would be nice of you. Do I go somewhere now to make the bail? She held out an official-looking piece of paper. "We're just putting up our deed as a property bond."

"No, that won't be necessary. Chester's getting what's known as a 'sheriff's O.R. release.' It means he's being released on his own recognizance. Kind of like a signature loan at the bank. He's being released on his honor that he will make all future court appearances."

"Thank you, Sheriff," said Chet, pleased that maybe someone finally believed him.

"Yes, thank you so much, Sheriff Roark. That's very kind of you."

"Just doing my job. Well, you two get on your way. I'm sure Brad is waiting for you."

Mrs. Buçek shot a glance at him, curious how he knew about Bradley, then put her arm on Chet's back to lead him out.

As Chet turn and stepped toward the door, he stopped. On the wall to the right was a shadowbox. Inside were mounted the Marine Corps eagle-anchor-globe device, the Rifle Expert badge, some other medals, and three rows of ribbons. He didn't know all of them but immediately recognized the Vietnam service ribbon. He turned around to look at the sheriff. Their eyes met.

"Tell your dad I said 'Semper Fi.'"

"Yes, sir. I will," Chet said as his mother kept him moving out the door.

There are two votes I can count on next election, the lawman decided. After they left, Sheriff Roark picked up his phone and pressed a button. "Martha, find out who's writing the report on that Buçek case and have him call me forthwith. I'll bet they never even interviewed the suspect."

"Are you sure you don't want to stay home today? Dad will be home around lunchtime."

"No, Mom. I've got perfect attendance going, and I can't miss practice. The state tournament is Saturday. Please write me an excuse for being tardy. Can I take the car to school? I'll bring Alexis home with me, if she wants to stay for my practice. I just want to take a shower and change clothes."

"That's fine. Just be real careful. There's still a lot of ice on the road."

Chet got to school in time to make his last morning class. The instant the bell rang, he hurried to the cafeteria to watch for Melanie.

He smiled as soon as he saw her walk in with her girl-friends, and the grin grew from ear to ear when her smile signaled she had seen him. She broke away from her friends and was walking toward him when two guys, juniors, walked by with their trays and loudly said "Chester the Molester" without stopping.

Chet turned at the sound of his name, but when they didn't stop, his attention went back to Melanie, who was now standing before him. He gently touched her swollen cheek with the back of his hand. It was badly bruised, despite her attempt to hide it with makeup.

"Chet, I'm sorry."

Befuddled, Chet said, "Sorry for what?"

She took his hand and started leading him toward the hallway, away from the lunchtime crowd. "The news," she said.

Chet smiled, unsure what she meant. "Melanie, what are you talking about?"

"The news crew out on the road yesterday afternoon. They took pictures of you, and me, and my dad, and even though none of us said anything, the sheriffs must have. Anyway, somehow they got your name. They probably recognized my dad from the State Farm commercial. Once they had his name, they tracked down mine. It was on the ten o'clock news last night and the morning news today."

"Yeah? Okay? What's the big deal?"

"They twisted the whole story, and now it's all over town that you raped me. I've been telling everyone I know that it's not true and how you saved my life."

Chet could barely hear her, the sickening feeling in his stomach was so great. But he didn't want Melanie to worry or blame herself.

"It'll be okay, Mel. You'll see. I don't feel like eating right now. Maybe I'll get a snack later."

He had never called her Mel before. She liked it. She wanted to hug him but simply squeezed his hand as they exchanged pensive smiles with each other, and then he left.

As he walked out of the cafeteria, he heard someone else call him Chester the Molester.

Alexis Buçek couldn't have been happier. Her dad was home safely and she was riding her horse. She loved winter days like this, cold and brisk with no wind to lower the wind-chill. She and Buckshot had left as soon as she got home from school, changed clothes, and brushed and tacked him up.

They were coming across the fallow field behind the barn on their way home and every time the dun gelding lifted his forelegs in the pristine snow, a spray of white flew out in front of them. Alexis saw a dark SUV, its lower half gray with salt and road grime, pulling into their driveway.

She rode into the yard just as a woman and a girl got out of the car with Chet's dog, Belle. Dual clouds of breath emitted from Buckshot's nostrils as Alexis pretended she needed to ride that direction just so she could see who they were. She didn't know the woman, but immediately recognized the girl.

She was a senior at their school, one of the cheerleaders, and the one in the picture from the school paper that Chet had hanging in his room, a review of the school's fall musical,

The King and I. Alexis even remembered the corny headline: "Melanie the Melodious." Her crazy brother had gone to both performances two weekends in a row.

"Hello," the girl said, which was echoed by the woman, probably her mother.

"Hello."

"Is your mother home?" asked the woman.

"Yes, she's inside."

The girl had walked toward her. Alexis had seen her from a distance at football and basketball games and once or twice in the cafeteria. Everyone at school knew she was cute, but seeing her close-up, Alexis saw she was truly pretty.

Alexis surmised she knew something about horses, too, because she didn't walk straight toward Buckshot's nose but approached at an angle so the horse would see her easily. Then, when the girl reached up and held Buckshot's headstall while she rubbed his nose, Alexis decided she did know something, even if it was impolite to do that without permission.

"Good-looking horse."

"Thank you."

"Quarter Horse?"

"Uh huh."

The girl let go of the headstall. "Is Chet home?"

"No, not yet. He's probably still at wrestling practice."

"Oh, yeah. That's right."

Alexis thought she looked disappointed.

"Come on, Melanie," said the woman. The two walked toward the back door of the house.

Sue Hondel had been baking Toll House cookies when Melanie came home. From the early time, Sue knew she'd gotten a ride from someone.

"Hi, sweetheart. Want a cookie?" she had asked while Melanie was hanging up her coat in the back hall.

"Mom, I don't know what do to," Melanie had declared as tears streamed down her face.

Sue had known Melanie wouldn't maintain her self-imposed exile and silence forever. Her kids always came back to her when they had a problem.

"What's the matter, angel?"

"You can't believe what that news on TV has caused at school and all over the Village."

"Because people think you were raped?"

"No, Mommy. They can think what they want about me. No, because they think Chet would do that to me. He saved my life, Mommy, and they're calling him Chester the Molester all over school."

Melanie had buried her head on her mother's shoulder and wept while her mom stroked her back. When Melanie had cried it all out, Sue had said, "Tell me the whole story and how we might make it better."

Ellen Buçek was in the kitchen preparing dinner when she heard someone knocking on the backdoor. She opened it and saw a woman and teenage girl. Belle shot by on a search of the house for Chet.

"Mrs. Buçek?"

"Yes," she said, not recognizing either of them or knowing what they might want.

"I'm Sue Hondel, and this is my daughter, Melanie."

That name immediately rang a bell. Ellen looked at the daughter, memorizing her face and comparing it to the brief shot she had seen on the news. She wiped her hands on the front of her apron and exchanged handshakes with both of them.

"May we come in for a few minutes?"

"Of course, please come in. And thank you for bringing Belle back."

The guests both politely wiped their feet on the rug in the hall. Sue Hondel saw the calendar on the hallway wall with the bottom section divided between the church schedule on one side and an ad for the local funeral home on the other. "Do you go to St. Anne's?" she asked.

"Yes, we do," replied Ellen, assuming the question was an ice-breaker more than a desire for information.

"I'm sorry we've never seen you. We usually go to the ten-thirty."

"Me, too. We just moved here before Labor Day. We attend the Extraordinary Form at nine. Let's sit in the dining room," said Ellen, leading the way.

"Whatever you're making smells good."

"Thank you. It's beef stroganoff, one of my husband's favorites."

Sue nodded her head knowingly.

"Oh, excuse me, honey, I didn't know you had company," said Peter Buçek, who happened to walk into the room.

"Peter, this is Sue Hondel and her daughter, Melanie."

"Mr. Buçek..." began Sue as she extended he hand.

"Call me Pete." He also shook the girl's hand, letting her address him as Mr. Buçek. He couldn't help but notice, despite the battered face, she was a wholesomely beautiful young woman.

"Would you have time to join us?" asked Sue. "I'd prefer you both heard us out." After they were seated, Sue continued. "Your son rescued Melanie Saturday afternoon and truly saved her life. Unfortunately, things were said and other things misconstrued."

The Buçeks listened to Melanie's retelling of the story and the effect the news story was having in town. Peter had watched the report because Ellen had the foresight to record it on their DVR, and, being a veteran litigator, he could tell Melanie was telling the whole truth, even the part about her own father. He was able to infer what the deputies may have said and how the television news had interpreted it to create a sensational scandal.

When both Melanie and her mother concluded by offering their separate apologies, Peter finally spoke. "It was really nice of you both to come out here and it was a pleasure to meet you both. But unfortunately, our son is the one who should be receiving the apology, not us, and it is *Mr.* Hondel who should be delivering it."

Melanie seemed sad that this visit wasn't going to make everything all right, but Sue nodded her head, acknowledging the truth of Pete's assessment.

After a little more small talk, they all said their good-byes as the Buçeks walked their guests to the door.

Chapter 14

Chet drove the family car into the garage and saw a Dodge Neon with a Budget sticker on the rear bumper parked at the backdoor. The rental car had to mean his dad was home. His assumption was confirmed as soon as he walked in the house. He smelled the beef stroganoff and knew it was his dad's welcome-home meal. By the time Chet had his coat off and shoes wiped, Peter Buçek was striding into the kitchen.

"Hi, Dad!"

"Hello, Chet!"

They exchanged a hardy handclasp until his father pulled him into a bear hug. "Darn, boy, you get taller and stouter every time I see you!"

Chet grinned with pride, on the verge of joyful tears that his dad was home safely, even for this short time.

"What happened to your hands?" asked Peter after seeing some Band-Aids on one hand, then examining broken and bruised skin on both.

"Oh, nothing."

Peter hadn't been in a fist fight in many, many years, but he knew the evidence when he saw it. Having heard Melanie Hondel's account of the situation in town, he imagined what may have happened. But there were more pressing matters tonight, so he didn't pursue the subject further.

Unknown to Chet, his father had ordered Alexis and Brad to their rooms as soon as he'd heard the family car crunching the snow and gravel on the driveway. Ellen remained in the kitchen, frosting a cake.

"Chet, I'm going to get right to the point. Mom has told me what happened as best as she knows it. I've watched the news report on the DVR." For the moment, Peter left out the retelling of the story by Melanie, not wanting Chet's mind to wander while they talked.

"I want you to tell me everything, every *single* thing, no matter how small or unimportant you think it is, that happened from the moment you knew that girl was in trouble until Mom brought you home this morning. No, until you came home from school today."

Chet retold the story again, but this time in more detail, in fact, in more vivid detail than he had told the sheriff or his mother. He and his dad had not discussed sex since he'd gotten the birds-and-the-bees story when he was twelve, although in the past year, his dad had included him in some double entendre or sexual innuendo jokes when his Marine buddies were around. But his father had asked for every detail, and he delivered, thankful that his father didn't show any sign of shock or disapproval.

For his part, Peter Buçek was no stranger to sex. Besides being happily married, as a Marine, he'd probably heard every story and joke, no matter how raunchy, that had ever been told. As a JAG officer, he had both prosecuted and defended crimes involving rape, sexual assault, and even a murder with a heavy sexual angle. Still, it was somewhat disconcerting for him to hear this young man, his son, tell him about the beauty of a girl's breasts or the color of her pubic hair. It seemed only yesterday he'd been teaching a little boy how to ride a two-wheel bike at Camp Pendleton.

When his son had finished, Peter had only one question. "Chet, I've never known you to lie, so you have a lifetime of credibility behind you. But you're a virile young man, an athlete, and I remember what was on my mind when I was your age. I just want to confirm, you were naked, skin to skin, with that girl all night and you never tried anything?"

Chet looked his father in the eye. "Dad, I won't fool you. The first part of the night, we were so cold, I never thought of it, even if I could've found my unit, as frozen as it was. The rest of the night, except for the accident I told you about, I had a woody buried in the mattress while we just lay together talking, trying to stay warm. Besides, Dad, she's not that kind of girl,...*and* I really like her."

Peter grinned at his son's honesty and choice of words. Having already heard Melanie's version of the same story, he thought, *Chet, you're either afraid to tell me or to admit it to yourself, but you more than like her.*

"Okay, Mom has already walked through here twice, giving me the eye, so I know she wants to serve dinner; I'll make this part fast.

"You've heard me speak of Rodger Harris, my best friend from law school. He's a State's Attorney in Cook County. He advised me on how best to put this horror story to rest. I spoke to Sheriff Roark this afternoon. He personally reviewed his deputies' reports in your case and recommended it not even be submitted to the State's Attorney. I asked him to do it anyway, along with a memo about his appraisal of the case.

"Rodger put me in touch with a prosecutor here in Winnebago County named Lee Williams. Remember what

I told you about networking being so important in the law? Anyway, after a call from Rodger, Mr. Williams expedited review of your case. He has also responded in writing that his office has rejected the case for prosecution. He then did us a big favor by using his good reputation with the court to get our case heard on tomorrow morning's court calendar."

"Our case? We have a case?"

"Your case, and mine as your attorney. We'll go straight there in the morning, then you can follow me to the rental-car place, and I'll drive you to school."

"Okay."

"Alexis! Bradley! Why isn't this table set? It's Daddy's first night back and you're trying to starve me to death!"

Feet could be heard stampeding down the stairs.

"Chet, help Mom get the meal on the table. By the way, did I mention that Melanie and her mother were here today?"

Chet's head whipped around in shock.

"They were?"

"I'll tell you all about it after supper."

"Ahhh, Dad!"

Peter allowed plenty of time for travel, finding a parking place, and getting through the security checkpoint in the county justice center, home of the county courts and various other county agencies. Despite the below-freezing temperature, the roads were dry with average weekday traffic. Huge mounds of plowed snow lined all the main streets. He opted for paid parking in a lot within a block of the courthouse, and the line through security moved smoothly.

Inside, Lieutenant Colonel Buçek took off his khaki all-weather topcoat, draped it over his left arm, and removed his barracks cover, the stiff green cap with black brim. Typical of airports, train stations, or any public place where the public congregates, a Marine in uniform, particularly an officer, drew attention. The looks ran the gamut from respect to curiosity to contempt and garnered the occasional acknowledging nod or "Semper Fi, Colonel" from former Marines.

Peter and Chet were two of the first people admitted into the criminal presiding department when the courtroom opened. The nameplate on the front of the bench said "Ernest N. Sharp, Judge." At eight-thirty, the bailiff announced in a loud voice, All rise." The din from the parties and spectators in the gallery and the attorneys who were sitting in the jury box or milling about inside the bar instantly subsided.

The judge walked in from a door off to the side of the bench and turned to the American flag. He was a lean man of medium height, with white hair and a long patrician nose and, Peter had learned, an aloof attitude to match. The bailiff then led the Pledge of Allegiance. Finished, he said, "Come to order, court is now in session. The Honorable Ernest N. Sharp presiding."

The judge walked up the three steps to the bench and sat in the tall-backed, black leather chair. He said, "Good morning, everyone," and all the attorneys and most of the public in the gallery responded with, "Good morning, Your Honor."

The bailiff went through the morning's calendar, first calling all the trials. Most of the attorneys for each side announced their presence and said they were ready. Others asked to "trail" for the arrival of witnesses or so they could continue negotiations toward a possible change of plea. Those who were ready were assigned by Judge Sharp to another courtroom elsewhere in the courthouse.

The bailiff then called all the preliminary hearings and they, likewise, were assigned out to courtrooms or trailed for what Chet heard was "second call."

Finally, Chet's matter was called. "Ex parte motion, In Re Buçek." Surprisingly, the bailiff pronounced their name correctly. Peter looked over and smiled at the bailiff, who smiled back with a look on his face as if to say, "What, you think I don't know how to pronounce Buçek?".

Chet left his coat on his seat in the gallery and followed his father through the swinging gate in "the bar," the little fence that separated the public from the judicial area. The judge looked up from reviewing their papers in front of him, then looked down at them.

"Who represents Chester Buçek?" He pronounced it Bewsek, despite his bailiff's cue.

"Good morning, Your Honor. Peter Buçek for the moving party."

The judge looked over at Chet, who was wearing dress pants, a white shirt, and a tie, then back at Peter.

"This is a civilian court, Colonel."

"That's correct, Your Honor."

"Is there a reason you're appearing here in your Class A's?"

Peter had learned in law school that a key to courtroom success was preparation. Preparation included gathering intelligence on the judge in front of whom one was likely to appear. State's Attorney Williams had warned him about Sharp's attitude and told him he was a retired Navy officer who prided himself on tradition, both naval and legal. Unfortunately, the judge had a reputation for being less than careful about other rules of law.

Mr. Williams said it was only because Peter was vouched for by Rodger Harris that he shared with him the local joke that the judge's middle initial stood for "Not-so." Reportedly, the reason his fellow judges had elected him to the presiding department was because all the attorneys hated him when he was in a trial department and used every available legal maneuver to avoid his courtroom.

After he had gotten off the phone with Rodger, Peter had gone online through his military data sites and learned that Judge Sharp had retired as a Lieutenant Commander in the Naval Reserves, one rung below Peter's current rank.

"Yes, Your Honor. I'm on active duty and entitled to wear my uniform."

"And you're a member of the bar of this state."

"Yes, Your Honor. This state, the Northern District of Illinois, all federal circuits, and the Supreme Court of the United States."

Realizing all legalities, procedures, and traditions had been complied with, and that he wasn't about to trip up this attorney, Sharp invited Peter to address his motion.

"As the court can see, this is a motion for a finding of factual innocence, destruction of the arrest record, and return of property. Exhibit One is a copy of a personal memorandum from Sheriff Randall Roark to the State's Attorney."

"Uh huh," said the judge, "I can see the sheriff was his usual pithy self."

"I'd like to invite the court's attention to Exhibit Two, in particular. You will notice, Your Honor, that Assistant State's Attorney Lee Williams not only rejected the case, as the Sheriff's Office anticipated, but also added additional comments regarding the lack of corpus, the absence of any admission, and the victim's statement that the battery was, in fact, inflicted by another individual. Finally, Your Honor, Exhibit Three is a declaration made under penalty of perjury by the moving party. An order is provided at the back."

Judge Sharp had been perusing each exhibit in order. Though only an abbreviation of the entire event, the declaration was longer, and he took a few minutes to read it thoroughly. Peter and Chet heard two or three "hmmms" as he read.

When he looked up, the judge addressed Chet. "Jumped in freezing water to save that young woman, then carried her to shelter and kept her alive through the night."

It was a statement, not a question, but Chet responded, "Yes, Your Honor."

"Well done, young man. I see no reason why this questionable citizen's arrest or other faulty conclusions in this matter should take up valuable space in the sheriff's office where they might come back to haunt you some day, nor why you shouldn't get your rifle back. The motions are granted."

The judge signed the orders, and his clerk conformed three other copies with official court stamps. The original would stay with the court. Chet and his father waited in the gallery until the clerk completed the minute order. The bailiff then handed them a copy of the minute order and the conformed copies: one for the State's Attorney, one for the sheriff's office, and one for the family's safety deposit box.

As they headed toward the courthouse exit, Chet said, "Thank you, Dad. You looked good in there."

Peter slapped his son on the back. "So did you."

Chet had removed his tie in the car, so as soon as his dad pulled up in front of the school, he jumped out with his book bag and gym bag. "Thanks again, Dad, and thanks for the ride. See you tonight,"

"Okay, Chet. Have a great day."

Elated at the way things had gone, Chet was bounding up the front steps of the school when a man in regular street clothes who had been standing near the doors stepped in front of him.

"Chester Buçek?"

"Yes, sir?"

The man, a process server, handed him two sheets of white paper stapled to heavy blue paper and folded in thirds. "You are hereby served with a temporary restraining order to stay away from one Melanie Hondel. All the details and your date to respond are contained in the order."

Without another word, he walked down the steps toward the street.

This was supposed to be all over with, thought Chet as he entered the building, reading the papers.

Chapter 15

Afternoon classes were changing when Kandy Kaegan, the head cheerleader, bounced up to Melanie while she and Mary Frances were at their adjoining lockers.

Kandy had been a cheerleader as long as anyone could remember. Her mother sent her to cheer camp every summer and the girl couldn't help herself, she just oozed school spirit. One always felt she was on the verge of a tumbling routine. The whole town knew her life's sole ambition was to end up in Dallas.

"Melanie, did you hear the news?" Then turning to Mary Frances as if she had suddenly materialized at that location and didn't know who she was, Kandy said, "Oh! Hi."

The school year's imminent class valedictorian, icicles dripping from her voice, responded, "Hello, Kandace."

Again oblivious to Mary Frances and not waiting for Melanie to answer, Kandy went on, "Our wrestling team qualified for the state tournament last Saturday and we get to go with them on the bus! Can you believe it, one more time to shake the pompoms and do the splits for our alma mater!"

Melanie thought about all the possibilities of that. "Okay, Kandy. I'll be there."

"You know we never cheered at a wrestling match before. Maybe I can come up with a special new routine."

"Sounds like a plan, Kandy. You do that."

After Kandy went bouncing down the hall, Mary Frances said, "If I hadn't known her my whole life, I'd think that girl was on speed."

No sooner had the future Cowboys cheerleader left than Gigi arrived.

"Did you hear the news?"

"Our wrestling team is going to state?" asked Mary Frances.

"Yeah," said Gigi, all disappointed. "How did you know?"

"Tigger, I mean Kandy Kaegan, just told us."

"Oh. Well, did you hear the pep band is going, too? Maybe we can sit together on the bus, huh, Melanie?"

Melanie figured it would be good to have a contingency plan if her daydream didn't come true. "Sure, Gigi, that'd be great."

"Uh oh, what's up now?" said Mary Frances.

Shannon came running up.

"Did you guys see Tommy Schmidt?"

"No," said Mary Frances. "I didn't have Automotive Shop last period."

"Why would I even want to?" asked Melanie. "I hope I never see him again."

"Well, then don't look now, 'cause he's coming right this way."

Mary Frances took a quick glance and couldn't believe what she saw. "Oh my God!" She turned and shared her shocked expression with Shannon.

Shannon was still facing his direction and whispered to her friends. "He's not just walking past. He's coming right here."

Even Melanie turned to see what he was up to as Tommy finished his approach. He was a big guy, at least six-one when he stood up straight, but he was walking with his shoulders stooped and his head hanging down. He was wearing his letterman's jacket with the two chevrons on the big D, denoting his third varsity letter. But his face looked like he'd been in a car wreck. One eye was an ugly purplish-black and completely swollen shut. His nose looked crooked. If it wasn't broken, it was still swollen to twice its normal size. Bruises and numerous scratches marked the rest of his head and face.

He ignored the others and walked right up to Melanie, almost to the point of invading her private space. Even in the midst of her friends and other students walking past, she felt intimidated.

"Melanie, I don't expect you to forgive me, but I want you to know I'm truly sorry for what I did last Saturday. I was totally out of line. I'm ashamed of myself and deserve every bit of the dirty looks I'm gettin' around school. You don't have to believe me, but I swear it's the truth, if I live to be a hundred, I will never hit another woman the rest of my life."

Without waiting for a reply, he turned and walked away, still hunched over.

"Well, that was a front seat in the living theater," said Mary Frances. "Almost like he memorized it, the phony piece of..."

"Mary Frances!" exclaimed Gigi, shocked at the expected expletive.

"...piece of human excrement."

"Probably did memorize it," agreed Shannon. "I wonder how he got so banged up."

"Oh, I think I know," said Melanie.

"Chet!"

He recognized the voice instantly but kept walking along the shoveled sidewalk toward the gymnasium building.

"Chet! Stop! It's me."

He stopped and turned, watching her jog toward him with her books. He looked both directions to ensure they were alone. They were alongside the gym wall, and no one else was around.

She came up close to him. Her nose and cheeks were already pink from the cold. He couldn't help but smile at her. The girl was totally cute.

She took his right hand and began pulling off his glove. He didn't resist, hungry for the physical contact.

She saw the bruised and battered knuckles. Without letting go of his hand, Melanie looked at him. "You didn't have to do that."

"Yes, I did. Boys don't hit girls."

She looked at him tenderly but slightly frightened by this violent side of him she'd never seen.

"Did he apologize to you in front of your friends?"

She nodded, still looking at him, noticing for the first time his face was totally free of any evidence of being in a fight.

"I meant you don't have to take care of me."

She may as well have stabbed him in the heart.

"I thought I did a pretty good job of taking care of you the other night."

She heard the hurt in his voice.

"No, not like that. I liked that...and I appreciated it. I meant you don't have to fight my battles for me."

"Sometime guys have to fight the battles for those who can't."

She nodded, knowing he was right. Wanting to change the subject, she said, "Some detectives came by during school yesterday afternoon and interviewed me. They said they were talking to Tommy next."

"Melanie, I really need to get going."

"Practice doesn't start for another fifteen minutes. I haven't seen you all day, and hardly at all yesterday."

"Mel, I can't be around you. You don't want me to get in trouble, do you?"

"What does that mean, you can't be around me?" The pique in her voice was obvious.

"You know, the restraining order."

"What restraining order?"

He could tell she didn't know.

"Your dad had me served with a restraining order today. I can't be within one hundred feet of you unless it's in school or by mere happenstance. I can't even call you on the phone, or contact you on the Internet, or through a third party."

She looked at him, dumbfounded and embarrassed.

"Chet, I'm sorry. I didn't know anything about it."

To lighten the tension, he teased her. "Of course, I can't get in trouble for contacting you because I don't have your phone number or e-mail, Facebook, or Twitter addresses."

The buses started queuing up.

"There's your bus. I have to go. Can I have my glove back?"

She realized she was still holding his hand. She looked at the scabbed knuckles, then kissed the palm of his hand and gave him his glove.

He put it on and smiled. "This will be over someday."

Melanie sat by some geeky sophomore on the bus so she wouldn't have to talk to anyone. She looked out the window until her stop, one of the early ones, came up. Before she was twenty feet from the bus stop, still alone, tears were landing on the books she carried in her arms in front of her.

Once in the house, she went straight to her room, not stopping to see what her mom was doing or to let her know she was home. She pressed the Power button on her computer and let it warm up as she changed out of the clothes she had worn to school. While waiting to get on her bus, she had texted Gigi, who she knew was friends with the wrestling team manager. Gigi texted back and said she had to wait while the manager called one or two of the guys on the team before he got what she'd asked him for.

Melanie typed in the e-mail address. On the subject line she wrote: NOW YOU HAVE TWO! The message was simply the 815 area code and the rest of her cell phone number. Below that, she wrote, "Be sure to read the school newspaper Thursday."

She stayed in her room, finishing her homework and talking to Shannon on the phone, until her mother called her for dinner.

Since Jack and Merrily had moved out, they no longer ate at the big dining room table. Instead, everyone sat at the dinette next to the window in the kitchen. Melanie's seat was directly across from her father's. She had such knots in her stomach about what she was going to say, and maybe do, that she had no appetite. She played with her vegetables and nibbled at the meatloaf until she couldn't stand the pressure inside.

"Dad, do you understand that if Chet hadn't been in the woods Saturday, I wouldn't be sitting here tonight?"

Her father, caught with food in his mouth, looked up, unsure what had brought this on, particularly his daughter's angry tone.

"I fell through an ice-covered lake. I don't know how long I was there, calling for help until I couldn't yell anymore. If I didn't drown, I would have frozen to death. Instead of sitting here eating mashed potatoes, you would have been welcoming guests after my funeral."

"Melanie, I think that's a little overdramatic," said her mother.

Melanie gave her a look as if to say, "This isn't about you," but her father said, "That's okay, Sue, let her talk."

"Chet, a boy I barely knew, jumped in the freezing water to save me. He pulled me out and carried me to his little cabin. Do you think either of us would have made it through the night in freezing, wet clothes?"

Hank Hondel didn't reply but continued to look at his daughter, giving her his full attention.

"Yes, Dad, we slept together, naked..."

Nancy's head whipped toward her sister, green peas falling from the fork halfway to her mouth, eyes as big as saucers, shocked to be hearing this for the first time and eager to learn more.

"...hugging each other all night, trying to stay warm. And whatever perverted things you want to imagine, nothing happened; he never tried anything all night. He treated me with respect the entire time. In fact, he got up throughout the night to make sure the fire didn't go out in the stove, and got me water, and fed me...."

Tears had already been running down her cheeks, but now Melanie had to stop to catch her breath and control the lump in her throat.

"Then after he saved my life and you had already attacked him, then humiliated him on television, you went and got a restraining order against him and don't even bother to tell me?"

"Hank, you didn't tell me anything about getting a restraining order," said his wife, obviously perturbed to just be hearing of it.

"I did it Monday morning before work, as soon as the courthouse opened. I had forgotten all about it."

"So here's the deal, Dad. You get that restraining order taken off Chet tomorrow morning, or don't expect me to speak to you again. Ground me, take away my allowance, don't let me use the car, don't help me with college, I don't care. But as soon as I turn eighteen, I *will* move out."

Hank Hondel had always been proud of this child's spunk and independent spirit. He heard the resolve in her voice. But he was a father, which also meant he was a peacemaker.

"Okay, I'll do it before work tomorrow."

If he had expected a thank you, he was mistaken.

"There's one more thing. You're going to go to Chet's house, not on the phone, not in the street, but at his house, and apologize for how you've damaged his reputation in town."

Hank was clenching his teeth, but he nodded affirmatively.

Melanie wasn't finished. "Finally, there's the matter of restitution."

"I thought you said the apology was 'one more thing?' But go on."

Having already conceded the main points, Hank surrendered to the last demand as soon as Melanie described it.

"Thank you, Daddy."

He nodded his head.

Melanie looked at her mother. "May I be excused?"

Sue Hondel, angry, tense, relieved, simply nodded assent.

"Me, too?" asked Nancy.

"Yes."

After they were alone, Hank said, "Boy, she's really taking this all too personally."

"Hank, sometimes you're just too blind to see the nose in front of your face. She loves him."

"She does? Well, he is a nice-looking boy and there's no doubt he's brave. She did tell me he's very smart, and I guess he was a gentleman with her."

"Hank, you old fool. Every girl wants a guy like her father. Those are things that attracted me to you."

Hank took his wife's hand. "Thank you, sweetheart. Though I'm not so sure about me in the smart department, lately."

Chapter 16

Henry Hondel pulled his car into the small parking lot near his office just as Bernice Keller, his loyal secretary, drove into the spot next to him. They never parked in front of the business on Center Road, always optimistic that those places be available for potential new clients.

They walked together to the front door, which Henry unlocked and held for Bernice. Bernice turned on the lights, turned up the thermostat, and went to the tiny kitchen area to hang up her coat, take off her boots, and start the coffeemaker.

Henry went to his office directly behind the dual-purpose office and waiting room where Bernice worked. He put his hat and coat on the coat tree in the corner, and sank into his chair.

He knew he needed to make amends somehow, but he didn't want go to their house. Why had he ever given in to a hormonal teenager? He was ashamed of what he'd done and the thought of going out there just added to his embarrassment. He tried to think of some face-saving way to make the call without feeling totally emasculated when it was over. Nothing came to mind and after wasting a half hour, he picked up the phone just before nine a.m. and punched in the number.

"Hello," answered a man's voice.

It's probably him, but I better not assume anything, thought Henry. "Good morning. Is Mr. Buçek there?"

"This is *Peter* Buçek," he said, implying other Mister Buçeks lived there.

"This is Hank Hondel, I think-"

"Oh, yes. Good morning, Mr. Hondel, I thought you might be calling." The tone indicated just the opposite.

Henry winced. *Okay, I'll take that as a slam. He figured I might not have the guts to call.*

"I was involved in a grievous incident with your son and..." He paused to best phrase the rest of his sentence but the half second delay was too long.

"Yes, 'grievous incident' is a fair description when a grown man assaults someone who was a minor two weeks earlier," Peter said in a voice used to being listened to.

Well, he's obviously not going to make this easy for me. "I won't be surprised if you turn me down, but I would like to come out to your home...any time of your convenience, of course...to personally apologize to your son. And if there were any medical costs, or even damages to his clothes from the water-"

Peter cut him off again. "Speaking of damages, I understand you're in the insurance business, Mr. Hondel. How large is the personal liability umbrella on your homeowners insurance? Surely, you have looked at it since this unhappy incident."

Henry felt his sphincter tighten. *God, he's coming after me for money.*

"I count at least five causes of action for civil damages. Let's see, assault, battery, negligent infliction of emotional distress for the humiliation of spending a night in jail and being the butt of jokes at school. Can you imagine what that does to a teenage boy?

"Then I think your statement, 'You hit my daughter,' in front of at least five witnesses, which, I might add, has never been withdrawn or corrected, constitutes slander. Of course, because all this bad publicity will likely affect my son's chances of college scholarships and future employment opportunities, I think interference with financial advantage would fly, as well."

Henry forced the words through his dry mouth. "You're planning to sue me?"

Peter hesitated on purpose. *Let him think about it for a moment.*

"No, sir, I am not. It seems my son has feelings for your daughter and would not appreciate me doing so. Let me say, as a father, the thought of money damages barely scrapes the surface. My first instinct was to find you and let you try having a piece of someone your own size. But for my reputation as an officer in the United States Marine Corps and a member of the Illinois State Bar, I may well have done so."

Henry didn't know what to say next. The guy wasn't going to sue him and wasn't going to punch him out, even though he considered it.

Before Henry could formulate another thought, the man continued. "Seven o'clock tonight would be fine with us, if that fits into your schedule."

"Uh, uh, sure, yes, of course, that would be fine. I'll see you then."

"You know where we're at, right?"

"Of course, the old Cleary farm. My wife was just there."

"We'll expect you at seven, then."

Peter Buçek hung up with neither of them saying good-bye.

Henry slumped back into his leather office chair, already dreading going out to the Buçeks' home. He looked down and noticed his hand was shaking.

It was Alexis' turn to wash the dishes and Brad's turn to dry that night. Chet went up to his room and started on his homework.

About a half hour later, the family heard Belle barking upstairs.

"Someone's coming. It must be him," said Peter Buçek.

Moments later, the family, too, heard the crunch of car tires on the gravel driveway near the house. Peter got up, walked to the foyer, and turned on the porch light.

Hank Hondel arrived a minute early. He turned off the engine and sat in the car for twenty or thirty seconds, still thinking about what he'd say, wondering how he would be treated and how his words would be received. After the less-than-cordial phone conversation that morning, he felt particularly vulnerable.

Mostly, he just felt foolish for letting his feelings get the best of him like they had. Usually, he was always in control of his emotions. Heck, he was an award-winning salesman. Aside from selling a great product, he made his living by being friendly and getting people to like him, or at least making them feel comfortable before he tried to sell them.

Oh well, gotta get this over with.

The car chime sounded when he opened the door, and he reached back to take the keys from the ignition. The porch light helped him choose his route toward the front door. A gust of bitter wind came around the house, causing him to pull up the zipper on his parka to the top, just as some snow blew off the roof, whipping his face.

He held onto the railing with his gloved hand as he climbed the five steps to the porch. He glanced up at the long icicles hanging from the eaves, then saw the blue star banner in the front room window, informing him a family member was serving overseas in a combat zone.

Instantly, he made the connection to the article he'd seen in the paper a few days earlier. *Oh great,* he thought, *the dad is a war hero, besides!*

Peter waited at the door but hesitated a moment after the knock so as not to spook their guest by opening it too quickly.

"Mr. Hondel?" he asked.

"Yes," replied the visitor, removing his hat and brushing his thinning hair down with his hand.

"Please come in." Peter stood to the side, holding the door, so the man could pass before he closed it.

Peter shook his hand. Mr. Hondel wiped off his feet on the mat in the foyer and entered the front room.

Hank looked around the comfortably furnished room and saw everyone except the person he had come to see: the mother in the living room, reading, a young boy who had been watching a television that had suddenly turned off, and a teenage girl in the next room on a computer.

"Let me take your coat," said Peter.

"No, thank you. I won't be staying long."

"Honey, kids, this is Mr. Henry Hondel. He has the State Farm insurance office in the Village.

"Mr. Hondel, this is my wife Ellen."

Ellen gave him a warm smile and said hello from her place on the couch.

"And our children, Alexis..."

Alexis stood up and said hi.

"...and Brad."

Brad waved.

"Can you show better manners than that, Bradley?"

The boy jumped to his feet. "Yes, sir. Sorry. Good evening, Mr. Hondel."

Peter Buçek went to the bottom of the stairs and called up. "Chet, there's someone here to see you."

Hank wouldn't have been surprised if the boy had kept him waiting out of spite, but he came right down, followed by the dog Melanie had brought to their house.

When Chet entered the living room, Hank approached. The dog made a move to sniff him but the boy snapped his fingers and pointed ahead and the dog obeyed.

"Hello, Chet. You probably remember me. I'm Hank Hondel, Melanie's father."

The boy accepted his extended hand and provided a firm, manly handshake, looking him in the eye the entire time. Henry guessed him to be about five-eleven, taller than he remembered.

"How do you do, sir? Is Melanie okay?"

This wasn't the way Hank had imagined the conversation beginning and was caught off guard.

"Yes. Yes, she's doing quite well. Thank you for asking."

Hank turned to Peter Buçek. "Is there someplace we could talk?"

Peter assumed, correctly, that the man meant himself and Chet.

"No, sir, I'm sorry. Right here will be fine. This has affected our entire family, and I think it only fair that they get to hear first-hand whatever you have to say to Chester."

The man was somewhat taken aback again but accepted his fate. "Er, okay. Chester, or do you prefer to be called Chet."

"Either one. Usually Chester is reserved for my grandpa."

Hank nodded in understanding.

"Okay. Chet, I came out here to apologize for everything I put you...you and your family...through. The things I did, the things I said, things I said out of anger without any basis whatsoever. I love all my children, but now, with Melanie soon to leave for college, I was so frightened and I guess just flew into a rage when I saw her face and learned someone had hit her, and... and because I thought it was you who had caused my wife and me so much worry.

"I know now that you saved Melanie's life. She's made us understand that she would have died in that lake if it hadn't been for you pulling her out at the risk of your own life and then keeping her from freezing all night.

"Son, er, I mean Chet, I'm ashamed for having judged you without knowing any of the facts and for any ridicule my actions caused you or your family. I am truly sorry."

He paused, finished. Chet hesitated a moment, then began.

"Mr. Hondel, Melanie is a wonderful young woman, so I know you and Mrs. Hondel did a great job raising her, probably because your folks raised you right. Do you think my folks haven't worked just as hard to bring me up to be a good person, too? Melanie said you warned her about boys like the one who tried to take advantage of her and hit her. Did you ever tell her that not all guys are like that? In this house, boys don't hit girls. If someone hurt my mom or sister, they'd have my dad and me and Bradley to deal with, but we'd find out the whole story first before we did anything."

The older man nodded in understanding of what the young man was saying.

"I accept your apology. I can live with the rest of it, I'm just glad I was there when Melanie needed help and that she's okay."

Chet held out his hand and the older man took it, looking him in the eye.

"There's one other thing, Chet. I wouldn't embarrass you by offering you a reward for saving my daughter, there's not enough money in the world, but Melanie told us you lost six of your pelts when you stopped to rescue her. I'd appreciate it if you let us reimburse you for that."

He pulled out a folded check from his shirt pocket and handed it over. Chet unfolded it and looked at it.

"Mr. Hondel, I can't take this! This is way too much."

"No, Melanie said those were prime winter pelts and you would have gotten fifty dollars a piece for them. Please take it."

Chet turned to his dad for advice. Peter nodded his assent.

"Thank you, sir. That was very generous of you."

Chet and Melanie's father shook hands once more, as Peter Buçek approached to see Hank to the door.

When they were alone in the front hall, he said, "Mr. Hondel..."

"Please call me Hank."

"Okay. Hank, I'm sure it took a lot for you to come out here tonight, but I really appreciate it. Yes, your apology meant a lot, but you helped me teach my boy a lesson about how men are supposed to behave when they make a mistake, and I want to thank you for that."

Hank looked at Peter and saw that he was sincere. For the third time, Hank didn't know what to say, so he just nodded in understanding.

Peter walked out onto the porch with their guest. "I understand you go to St. Anne's."

"Uh, yeah, that's right."

"Ever go to their fish fries on Friday?"

"Nearly every week. Gotta rub elbows with my clients, make new contacts."

"I'll be home for a couple of weeks. Let's all sit together sometime."

"Sure. That'd be great. I'll tell the wife."

Chet arrived early, not wanting to miss Melanie before school started. He didn't know if she would be getting a ride with friends or taking the bus, which might affect which door she used. He bet on the main entrance and won. She got off the bus with two of her friends. The trio was gabbing away when he approached.

He knew girls must have some kind of special "girl manners" or something, because he'd seen it before. When a guy walks up to a girl who is surrounded by her friends, the friends will excuse themselves and keep walking if they know she's interested in the guy. But if she doesn't care for him, her friends shield her like a gaggle of spinster chaperones. He was fortunate to be in the former category.

After the two friends told Melanie they would see her later, he said, "Hi."

Melanie smiled back demurely. "Hi."

"I was reading the school paper while I waited."

"Yes. And..."

"And I saw your article."

He held up the latest four-page edition. The front page feature had the largest headline.

How Chester Buçek Saved My Life
by Melanie Hondel

"You have a talent for writing. Maybe you're the one who should be going into journalism."

"Well, four years of Honors English should be good for something. I understand there's a nice article in the Sports section about the wrestling team going to state, along with some beefcake photograph of a certain senior."

"Yep, I saw that, too," he said, blushing. "I don't know how you pulled that off in one day." He saw she again had the impish look he loved.

"My friend Mary Frances is editor of the paper."

He shook his head in understanding, appreciating that Melanie had done that for him. "I got your e-mail last night about the restraining order going away. Thank you."

"I didn't know how late you stayed up or when you went online, so I'm glad you got it."

"Your dad came over last night."

"I know."

"Did he tell you about it?"

"No."

"He was very nice. Told me he was sorry for what happened..."

"Did you accept his apology?"

"Of course. He's your dad."

She smiled, appreciating the consideration.

"But I would have anyway, just because it was the right thing to do."

"And you always do the right thing?"

"I try...sometimes better than others."

They stood there smiling at each other, feeling the chemistry between them but knowing they each had steps they needed to take in this courting dance they had begun.

"Your dad gave me a check, too. I tried to refuse, but he insisted. I suspect you had something to do with that, too."

Her grin was the only confirmation he needed.

"Thank you."

"Well, maybe you have enough to take me for pizza one of these nights, now that I know wrestlers eat pizza."

He smirked. *Now she's trying to make it easy for me,* he thought. *Is she afraid I don't know how to do this?*

"I heard the cheerleaders will be riding on the team bus to the state wrestling tournament Saturday..."

"Yeah, how come you never told me last Saturday that you qualified for state?"

"Like, maybe I was too busy saving your frigid little butt to think about it!"

She laughed out loud. "Fair enough."

"Anyway, as I was saying, maybe if a certain cheerleader sat with me on the bus, she'd bring me good luck in the tournament and I'd repay her by taking her out for dinner, pizza or whatever, when we got back."

Melanie smiled. "I think that could be arranged."

Sorry, Gigi. Guess you'll have to sit with someone else, she thought. *Plan A just went into effect!*

"And if my luck held, I might find out that person hadn't been asked to the St. Valentine's Day dance yet."

Melanie couldn't stop grinning. "Boy, that's pushing the luck thing pretty far. I'm not sure it'll last *that* long."

Chet grinned back. "Can I carry your books to your locker?"

"No, thank you," she said, then smiled the instant she saw the look of disappointment on his face. "But you can hold my hand."

Afterword

Did you know?

- About one in three high school students have been or will be involved in an abusive relationship.
- Forty percent of teenage girls ages 14 to 17 say they know someone their age who has been hit or beaten by a boyfriend.
- In one study, from 30 to 50 percent of female high school students reported having already experienced teen dating violence.

If you are the victim of dating violence or know someone who is, help is available from the groups listed below. There may be additional resources in your own state or community.

The National Teen Dating Abuse Helpline is a national 24-hour resource that can be accessed by phone (1-866-331-9474 and 1-866-331-8453 TTY) or the Internet, specifically designed for teens and young adults. The Helpline and **www. loveisrespect.org** offer real-time one-on-one support from trained Peer Advocates.

If you know or suspect a friend or fellow student is in an abusive relationship:

- Be specific about why you are concerned, e.g., "I saw a boy push you hard. Is he your boyfriend? Why did he do that?"
- If the student <u>does not</u> want to discuss this, encourage him / her to talk to a trusted adult (e.g., parent, school guidance counselor, Diamond Girl Leadership Coordinator / Mentor, or Best Men Leadership Coordinator / Mentor).
- Give the student the National Domestic Violence Hotline number – 1-800-799-SAFE.
- If the student <u>does</u> want to talk, do not criticize or attack the abuser. Ask, "What can I do to help?"
- Make sure the conversation is reported to the school guidance counselor immediately.

Other advice is available from the Best Friends Foundation. Check out the tips at **http://www.bestfriendsfoundation. org/BFSafetyRules.html**.

The U.S. Department of Health and Humans Services' Women's Health website (**http://www.womenshealth.gov/ violence/types/dating.cfm**) also offers a wealth of information and contacts, including such subjects as:

- Healthy Relationships vs. Unhealthy Relationships.
- Signs to help you know if you are being abused.
- How to get help for sexual assault and abuse.

Made in the USA
Las Vegas, NV
08 January 2024